Chapter One

ASH

I always wondered if I was supernatural enough to live in Willow Lake.

The town was unlike anywhere else. It wasn't a secret supernatural sanctuary—not exactly, anyway—but it was close. The ratio of supes to humans here was around three to one now, and the supe side was growing all the time. It was one of the reasons I liked it here so much. I might stick to humans for sex—back when I still had sex with people—but too many of them in a community was never a good thing.

I really shouldn't be so judgmental; my best friend and my boss were both human, after all. But the differences between supes and humans were just so... *obvious*. I suspected if more humans knew about us and how they weren't the most powerful species on the planet, their sense of peace would be shattered. Realizations like that tended to make humans stabby.

Honestly, I found it surprising *any* humans stayed in Willow Lake long, because even a weak-assed supe like me emitted a certain amount of magical energy. Humans, so I'd been told, got uneasy when surrounded by too many of us. Eventually their feeble senses finally registered the high magic levels and their brains started shouting *Danger! Run!*

Not that I was much of a predator by any definition of the word, but whatever.

Sure, I was technically a fire mage, but I couldn't do much. Turning my bedroom lights on and off without having to get out of bed wasn't particularly awe inspiring, not when anyone with the right gadget could clap and do the same thing.

Worse, sometimes I sensed *something* bigger and brighter lurking under my skin, and it just felt so damn familiar and wonderful that I knew it had to be my magic, but then I'd burp or sneeze or—and I will deny this to my dying breath—fart, and the feeling passed. So, it was probably just allergies… or gas. Which was awkward, right? Like, *Pardon me, but I might do something magical, or I might let out a silent and deadly one, so maybe don't stand so close.*

So, yeah… Not exactly brimming with magical oomph. Not anymore.

It sucked.

And being surrounded by werewolves like Hayden, hellhounds like Van, or mermen like Weston didn't help my self-confidence. As shifters, those guys oozed magic. It lived within the very fabric of their bodies. If they didn't have a healthy and strong magic, they couldn't exist.

HELLHOUNDS NEVER LIE

Willow Lake Supernaturals

Book 1

LORI AMES

Hellhounds Never Lie by Lori Ames

Published by November Snow
Copyright © 2023 by S.L. Paton. All rights reserved.
Digital edition / 2023 - ISBN 978-1-989764-60-2
Print edition / 2023 - ISBN 978-1-989764-61-9

Cover by: S.L Paton
Beta Reading by: Kirk Waite at Rare Bird Beta Reading

Thank you for respecting the hard work of this author.
loriames.com

And, well, without much magic, I didn't exactly excel, but at least I survived.

Oh, yeah, and I could talk to magical, non-shifter cats, so there was that. Although I hadn't met a supe in Willow Lake who couldn't, so it wasn't exactly an indicator of something amazing.

The first time it'd happened, I was sitting in the middle of the pub at the Willow Lake Inn during a busy Friday night. I'd only been in town for a few weeks, and everyone said the pub was the place to go to meet people. I'd just taken my first sip of my first pint when a fluffy calico cat —its furry coat a chaotic jumble of black, orange and white, with a black patch over one eye making it look like a pirate—jumped up on my table. The cat was on the chunky side, so he landed with a loud thump. It surprised the shit out of me.

My first thought after I realized it was a cat: Weren't animals on tables some kind of health code violation?

Then the cat had introduced itself—or rather himself, since he'd clearly given his pronouns.

I hadn't been prepared for that. I mean who would be?

But that was my only excuse for why my full pint of beer slipped from my fingers, crashed to the worn wooden table, and spilled *everywhere*. My pants and the front of my shirt were soaked through, but the most memorable part was the way the cat had yowled and jumped away like I'd stepped on its Halloween colored tail. Everyone—and I mean literally every single person in the pub—turned to stare at me like I was a monster for making the cat scream.

Pawington the Third, or Paws as the locals called him, had spent the rest of the night cleaning his fur—a bit excessively if you asked me—and scowling at me from across the room.

It'd taken two months before Paws had approached me again. Now, just over three years later, I couldn't get rid of the creature.

"Seriously," Paws said as he whipped his tail through the air, "how much longer will it take the kid to figure this shit out? My day on the betting pool is coming up soon and he isn't showing any sign of getting his shit together."

Paws never shouted, so I had to lean over and concentrate to hear him over the loud music playing on the old school jukebox, the clack of balls on the pool table, and the raucous conversation at the next table. I suspected the loud group was made up of chipmunk shifters, but without my magic at full capacity I couldn't be sure.

My conversation with Paws would be so much easier if I could pop a shimmering dome of silence over us like my mother did in situations like this. She had an affinity for air though, so even if my magic was full and normal, as a fire mage, I wouldn't have been able to do it.

"He's only been here a year. Give him a break." I glanced over at Jake, the new-ish owner of the Willow Lake Inn and Pub, as I adjusted my fuzzy pink sweater, tugging the collar of the shirt I wore under it, so it was between the itchy cashmere and my neck again. Cashmere was softer than the other types of wool I'd tried, but it still irritated the shit out of my skin. Being cold ninety-nine percent of the time sucked. Even during the hot spell we'd been going through, I was still cold. People looked at me like I was crazy, bundled up in long sleeved sweaters when everyone else was walking around in shorts and muscle tees. But I'd been this way since that one night several years ago—

Paws harrumphed, interrupting my thoughts, and glowered at Jake.

Ulric, Jake's grandfather, had left the place to him in his will last year. At first all the supes kept coming to the pub because it was their local and they figured any grandkid of Ulric's must be a supe too. When it became obvious the new guy couldn't see past the magical glamour most of his patrons wore to hide their non-human appearances, Jake had become the center of a big guessing game —with money involved, obviously—for when he'd realize he was a supe and finally see the rest of us for what we were.

Someone could expose him to the supernatural world in a way he couldn't ignore, which would allow him to see around all the glamours, but they'd forfeit their money. But, let's face it, Willow Lake didn't have a lot of entertainment; no one wanted to ruin the fun. So, as much as Paws complained and acted like he was ready to end it all and reveal everything to Jake, no one took him too seriously.

Jake looked over at me then, probably sensing he was being watched, and smiled.

No doubt about it, the guy was cute in a twink-ish kind of way. It was too bad I wanted a burly giant of a man— someone who could wrap me up in a big bear hug and cuddle—because Jake was nice. He was exactly the kind of guy my mother wanted me to fall for, the kind I'd always ignored in the past, the kind who wouldn't be dangerous. Although maybe it was premature to say he wasn't dangerous since no one knew what his supernatural abilities might be, assuming he had any.

I sighed and rubbed my chest to ground my thoughts, tracing one of the thick corded scars marking my chest through my layers of clothes. The scars occasionally itched, but they didn't hurt anymore. Touching the thick scar tissue, however, had become a habit, although probably not a healthy one.

When Jake's attention turned away from me, I let my gaze drift over the rest of the locals in the pub. There were a couple of guys who I wouldn't mind dragging home for the night, but... I frowned. I couldn't quite muster the nerve to actually approach them for a date. At this point, I wondered if I ever would.

A phantom ache shot through my scars.

Paws swatted my cheek. "Are you listening to me?"

The creature narrowed his yellow eyes as he tracked where my fingers were still moving over my scar. The weight of his curiosity had me yanking my hand away.

Nope. I didn't want to talk about my failed attempts at love with a cat, even a magical one. I didn't even want to think about my disastrous love life right now.

"Yeah, yeah. You didn't have to hit me." I rubbed where his claws had struck me, then pulled my hand away to look at it. Luckily, Paws hadn't drawn blood. It still stung though. "You want to win the bet. I get it."

Paws lifted his head and sniffed dismissively at me.

Some people got annoyed with the supernatural creature when he did arrogant things like that, but I was just thankful he wasn't pressing for answers about my scars. He was a nosy bastard, which he blamed on his feline nature, but I didn't buy that excuse. Paws was just a regular old snoop. He liked to know everything about everyone. Which meant he had to have made a few deductions about my past and he was biding his time before asking pointed questions to confirm his suspicions.

But, to my relief, he seemed happy enough to talk about Jake today.

My phone pinged. I glanced at it and grinned. Jeremy, my best friend—yes, the human one—had sent me a meme with a calico cat being snotty. Jer was a cat lover and had a seemingly endless supply of cat memes. Still, the timing on this particular one was perfect. I showed it to Paws, who hissed at the screen. I laughed and fired back a meme to Jer that I'd found earlier when I was on a break at the restaurant. He replied immediately.

MyBestestBFF4ever: Do you think a skilled barber could groom a sasquatch well enough that people would just think he was a really hairy man?

Me: Yep. Your last BF Steve was one.

MyBestestBFF4ever: Shut up. He was never my boyfriend. We went for coffee twice.

Me: He was very, very hairy and had that weirdly big forehead. And you said he grunted the whole time. Ergo, sasquatch.

MyBestestBFF4ever: Hmm… Now that you say that. *thinking face emoji* Maybe I should give him a call.

I knew for a fact Steve wasn't a supe, so I wasn't doing

anything that'd jeopardize his identity. Still, for someone who didn't know supes existed, Jeremy spent a lot of time speculating about supernatural creatures. I usually answered with the truth, even if he'd never know, but sometimes I pretended I was just as ignorant of supes as he was. After all, he wasn't asking because he wanted to out the supernatural community. No, he was just a guy with a vivid imagination who enjoyed thinking about what if scenarios.

And, for the record, he is the one who changed his name in my phone to MyBestestBFF4ever. At the time, I'd pointed out he didn't need the second F if he had the 4ever, but he was adamant. It was just so Jeremy. It made me smile whenever it popped up on my phone.

When he didn't text anything more, I put my phone down. Paws immediately lifted his head and started complaining again.

"Have you been listening to me?" Paws prodded. "Do you know how ridiculous it is to talk to a guy every day and have him meow back at you? But the fucking baby talk is the worst. Do I look like a damn baby? I'm telling you, I'm going to stuff a dead mouse in his mouth in the middle of the night if he keeps up with this bullshit."

"It's weird though, isn't it? That he doesn't have a clue about supes or his own power, whatever it is." I studied Jake again. "Maybe he isn't part of Ulric's blood line."

"Nah. That's Ulric's grandkid alright. Spitting image of him when he was the same age. And Hayden said he smells like Ulric's kin."

"I bet a better mage than me would be able to tell if he's been cursed or something."

"Stop that." Paws hit my face again.

"Would you quit doing that?" I glared at him.

"You've got power. I know you do. You just need to learn to use it."

And not have anyone steal it from me.

But I didn't say that part out loud.

I hadn't told anyone about what had happened to me before I moved here. It was too personal. Too humiliating. All the supes in town probably knew I was a little fucked up—most of them had intensely sensitive senses of one kind or another. You couldn't hide much from this many supernatural beings. But no one asked and I hadn't volunteered anything.

Knowing I could keep my secrets, and no one would bother me about them was one of the reasons I'd stayed. Although, with everyone so willing to happily ignore my secrets, they must have had a lot of practice. It made a person wonder what other skeletons were buried in people's closets... Still, if I wanted to keep mine, I couldn't expect everyone else to blab about theirs.

And I did want to keep my secret. More than anything.

I didn't want anyone to look at me the way I knew they would if they discovered my magic had been drained out of me like someone sucking up sawdust with a shop vac. And, if my magic hadn't recovered after all these years, I doubted it ever would. I couldn't handle everyone looking at me like the poor little broken mage I was.

Blah, blah, blah. *Woe is fucking me.*

Moving on.

It didn't help to live in the past and daydream about what I'd lost. I'd moved to Willow Lake to get away from my mother's constant coddling and my big brother's over-protectiveness. I didn't need to wallow in that shit anymore. And I didn't need to have the whole community look at me with pity.

I may be a broken mage, but no one here cared.

Paws whacked me in the face again. "I told you to stop that."

"Quit hitting me." I rubbed my cheek but before I could look for blood again, a loud crash from across the room made me jump. An unfamiliar energy surged through the room. I swore even the fibers in my sweater quaked.

"What the—?"

Paws had already jumped off the table and was running for the bar. With an athletically graceful leap I hadn't known the chunky creature was capable of, Paws was on top of the bar, weaving between beer taps and pint glasses. The few people who were seated along the counter were staring at Jake. Others, some of the regulars, were swapping money, probably thinking today was the day Jake would discover the supernatural world and wanting to get in a few last wagers.

A couple of humans in the crowd laughed and clapped, thinking someone had broken a tray of glasses and they deserved a good ribbing for it. They didn't seem to notice every supe in the place had stopped what they were doing to identify if the strange magic surging through the room was friendly or not. Humans were dumb like that.

Well, to be fair, very few of them knew they were surrounded by supes and magic.

"Distract the humans," Paws shouted, which would sound like a cat's meow to anyone not in the know.

The people closest to the humans jumped into action, but I followed Paws to the bar. I wasn't sure if I could help, but I was one of the few witches in town and sometimes my kind could help channel other magic. Even a weak and damaged magic like mine could be a conduit for someone else's. My former coven—or I guess it still was my coven since I hadn't formally demitted from it—did this all the time for one another. When mages linked up, each person in the chain amplified the magic a little more at very little magical expense.

The least I could do was offer, if needed.

Behind the counter, Jake was frantically rummaging through the drawer under the cash register. I might not be a were-creature and thus able to scent emotions, but even I could feel the tension rolling off the guy. When Jake wrapped his hands around a pen and a roll of register tape, he groaned like he'd just had the best orgasm and his shoulders relaxed. He unraveled a length of paper, not seeming to notice when the rest of the roll dropped over the counter and unspooled across the sticky tiled floor.

Jake jerked the pen over the paper in quick rapid strokes. His eyes seemed focused on a bottle of Amaretto on the wall, but his pen never slipped beyond the narrow limit of the paper. Not once. It was a bit creepy to be honest. He didn't blink. I wasn't even sure he was aware of what he was doing or looking at. I'd heard Jake was an artist and I had even thought about joining one of the art afternoons he organized for anyone who wanted to try their hand at doing something artistic, but I didn't think this was his usual method or medium.

Paws leapt from the serving counter to the back

counter where Jake was. He prowled toward the guy. Slowly. Silently. He moved like a deadly panther stalking its prey through the jungle. I didn't know exactly what Paws was—the creature might look like a house cat, but he was more than that. A lot more.

When Paws got within a foot of Jake's mad creation, he tilted his head and eyed the drawing.

"Hellfire and brimstone." Paws whipped his tail through the air. "He's a fucking oracle."

Surprise rippled through the pub. A few people picked up their phones and started texting or phoning their friends. This was big news. Everyone in Willow Lake would know about Jake in about fifteen minutes or less.

"Do you think he knows?" Sally, one of the regulars who was seated at the bar, asked.

"Nope." Paws popped the 'p.' "He still can't see us so he's obviously in denial. Believe me, I live with the guy. I'd know if he'd figured this shit out."

Jake didn't acknowledge the conversation. Had he even heard it? Was he in a trance? The whole situation was eerie. Everyone inched closer, curious to know what the oracle would share. I had never met an oracle before, but it was common knowledge their messages could be cryptic.

Finally, the pen dropped from Jake's hand. His fingers spasmed. He blinked. Then all the color drained from his face. He swayed for a moment before turning and bolting toward the bathroom.

"Weston," Paws shouted.

"On it," the merman said as he shot after Jake.

Weston was trained in first aid, so it made sense Paws had sent him after Jake. The vision had Jake looking a little queasy. Was this his first vision ever? If it was, hopefully the next one didn't take so much out of him.

As Alice, Jake's part time waitress, hurried behind the bar to fill in for him, Paws padded over to the drawing of Jake's vision. As soon as his yellow eyes took in the details, he swore.

"Hayden," he called out to the werewolf who refused to be called alpha, "what is the phase of the moon tonight?"

"Waning gibbous. The last quarter is tomorrow night. The new moon will be here at the end of next week," the werewolf answered without having to think about it. It always surprised me how in sync shifters were to nature, when I had enough trouble remembering the day of the week.

"Houston, we have a problem," Paws said. Then he ripped the drawing from the roll of paper with his teeth and picked it up in his mouth. He leapt off the counter, then carried the message to the far side of the pub, away from where the other supes had inconspicuously herded the humans. He placed the long narrow drawing on one of the small round pub tables.

As much as everyone was curious to see what had been drawn, no one moved except to get out of Hayden's way as he crossed to the table. The wolf may not like it when people called him their alpha, but that's what he was. And the fact he was the first to assess what Paws called a problem just showed he was our de facto leader regardless of what title he went by.

He looked like he'd come straight from his mechanic shop. A smudge of black grease still marred his cheek. His jeans, filthy with who knew what, strained over his ass as he bent over to look at what was scribbled on that bit of paper. I looked. Of course, I did. I think the whole bar did. The man had a great ass.

Whatever he saw made him growl.

"It might not happen right away..." Paws said.

"But we can't take the risk it won't," Hayden finished for him.

The next person to elbow their way to the table was Van. The hellhound was the Chief of Police on the local police force. I liked knowing Van had been chosen for his job based on his skills and experience—both supernatural and otherwise—by the Supernatural Council. The SC always stepped in when more than fifty percent of a population was supernatural and took measures to ensure the special police division was comprised of predominantly supernatural beings. Van had been promoted to Chief right around the time I moved to town. I suspected there was magic involved to keep the humans from questioning things, but I didn't care enough about the logistics to confirm my guess. I was just happy to have Van there when we needed him.

And, well, it probably didn't hurt he was hot as fuck with his dark skin and dark expressive eyes—I was pretty sure he could simply look at someone and they'd fall into bed with him. Then again, it seemed like most supes in town were good looking. Or maybe everyone appeared sexy to me because it'd been so long since I'd been with anyone, even a human.

Okay. I could admit it, I might fantasize about *all* these guys, but I would never do anything other than look at my fellow Lakers. I might drool over all the supes, but on the very rare occasions I actually had sex, I preferred my partners to be regular old humans. It was safer that way.

But how Van managed to deal with any of the humans in the community was anyone's best guess. They were a strange group. But we supes were happy to have one of our own as the guy in charge. After all, there were some things that couldn't be dealt with through the human justice system.

Van's lips flattened into an unimpressed scowl, then he nodded sharply.

"I'll deal with it," Hayden said. "It's my problem."

Hmm… That must mean the oracle's message was about wolves.

"We don't know the location," Van said. "Or even when it'll happen."

"It'll be by the new pack lands." Hayden shrugged like it was obvious. Then he pointed at the top of the scrap of paper. "And that says it'll be next week."

It was weird how the pack in the hills had been there for over a decade and people still called it new.

"There are too many roads for you to hit them all. We'll need more of us out there looking." Van crossed his arms. "Besides, you shouldn't be out there alone."

"Fine," Hayden snapped. Anger made his eyes flash gold, showing his wolf.

Hayden's history with the so-called new pack was a sore spot. After all, the new pack used to be Hayden's old pack before a bunch of them decided to follow his brother and leave town. It all happened before I moved to Willow Lake, but people talked about what happened like it was just last week. That, at least, wasn't a secret. Younger than Hayden and rumored to have been spoiled his whole life, Robbie was one messed up wolf—a purist who believed any supernatural who wasn't a wolf should be kicked out of Willow Lake. And humans? They shouldn't exist. Period.

The very idea of that kind of bigotry made energy surge in me until I wanted to sneeze. Or burp. Or—ahem —something else. Which, again, I really, really hoped wasn't me being gassy.

But seriously, anyone who believed bullshit like that didn't belong in our community. Hayden and the town as a whole were better off without them. It was too bad our alpha wolf still believed he'd failed those same assholes who'd renounced him as their leader.

Stupid prejudiced jerks.

From what I heard, no one—not his brother Robbie or anyone else—had even tried to challenge Hayden to become alpha here. They'd obviously known none of them, not even their new leader, would be able to take him. But that didn't mean they hadn't damaged Hayden.

Some hurts were just hidden. I knew all about that.

"We have a few days to sort this out. I'll come up with a schedule. We'll divvy up the roads, so we don't miss any," Van was saying, but I wasn't paying much attention now.

I was more curious about seeing what had the others so worried. I edged closer until I could make out the details. Considering the drawing was created with a plain ballpoint pen, it was clearer and more refined than I'd expected.

Under a dark sky with only a sliver of a crescent moon

visible was a group of fierce looking werewolves chasing down another creature. The wolves looked feral. With their elongated teeth bared, their hackles raised, and their claws ripping into the dirt, they raced over the land in their pursuit. But the creature in the front clenching a bag in their long intimidating teeth, that was who caught my eye. My chest tightened at the look in their eyes. Determination and resignation, maybe? I wasn't quite sure. But it was intense. Their fur looked like fire and it seemed to glow in the dark forest.

It had to be a hellhound. I was sure of it. I'd never seen Van shift, but I knew this wasn't him. It was someone new, someone who obviously needed help.

The image sent a chill down my spine.

Before I even realized I'd made a decision, I opened my mouth and said, "I'll go too."

Chapter Two

DILLON

Disappointment blanketed me as I glanced around the dingy old basement rumpus room with its dirty, harvest gold shag carpet and '70s brown wood paneling. It wasn't so much the room that bothered me, but the unkempt and boorish wolf pack who were using it as their meeting hall.

This pack wasn't the haven for supernatural creatures I'd been led to believe. Not even a little bit. In fact, I would go as far as to say it was the most backward, narrow-minded, self-centered, prejudiced group of supes I'd ever met. And that was saying something.

I should have known a supernatural utopia was too good to be true.

At my age, I also should have known better than to eavesdrop on people and think I'd come away with anything useful. But when I'd been sitting in a downtown café in the largest city in this part of the country and heard two people talking about this place, I'd needed to know more, because even if a small part of what they had said was true…

A chorus of discordant howls interrupted my thoughts.

"Tomorrow night we will embrace our savage beasts and be free again," Rob, the alpha, shouted enthusiastically at the others, building the pack's energy to a frenzied level.

I'd seen human leaders do similar things to their followers: Build adrenaline and excitement in the masses and then set them loose to cause havoc. Nothing good ever came from shit like that. Right now, emboldened by Rob's example, most of the pack had partially shifted and tilted their wolfed-out faces upward to bay at the water-stained ceiling. It was deafening in the confined space. The dulled pain in my head, which had arrived a few days ago when I'd first started to give up on this place, sharpened.

I sighed.

This was what I got for having a silly yearning to find a place to settle. It'd been a long time since I'd had people to call family; you'd think I'd have gotten used to being alone by now. Instead, my stupid dream got me into situations like this.

Whatever I'd hoped for—Family? Friendship? A place to call home?—it didn't matter, because this place was not a utopia. What was the opposite of utopia? Anti-utopia? That didn't sound right. And dystopia seemed more apocalyptic than what I was facing. I mean the world wasn't ending because these wolves were shitty people.

Well, whatever a non-utopia was called, this was it.

I'd been living with this pack for six days. Six fucking days! And I wasn't going to last another. Whatever new moon celebrations the pack did tomorrow night wouldn't include me. I'd be gone before then.

I didn't fit in here. Here or anywhere, apparently.

I sighed again.

I doubted there was a way to salvage the situation, but I should try, right?

"Can you explain, sir?" It went against my instincts, but I hunched down in my seat as I asked my question.

The wolves were already uneasy around me because of my size, but by questioning their alpha, I knew things could go sideways for me real fast. I didn't need them thinking I was challenging him for leadership. The last thing I wanted was to be the leader of a bunch of narrow-minded wolves in the middle of the boonies.

Don't get me wrong, I could take their alpha in a fight —shifted or not—but if I killed the idiot, then I'd have the dubious honor of being their next alpha. Wolves like this would never listen to a hellhound. They only respected their own kind.

But if I wanted to find out what was going on, I needed to play the game and pretend as though Rob was a good leader who needed to explain things to me as if I was stupid. I was still a member of the pack, after all. Even if I doubted I would be for much longer. As an alpha, he should want to incorporate me into his flock. I doubted he'd do much to enlighten me though. His kind usually preferred half-truths and bravado.

I couldn't believe I'd agreed to obey this guy when I'd joined. Yeah, it wasn't my smartest move.

I mean, I was a laid-back kind of guy. Someone once likened me to a sea urchin—even though my hellhound would never willingly step into a pond, let alone an ocean. But I guess maybe I was a little prickly when it came to letting people close, even though all I wanted was the terrestrial equivalent of a little tide pool to call my own. At least I thought that's what they were getting at when they described me that way; I'd never had any desire to go near the sea, so I didn't know a lot about the animals there.

Unfortunately, my relaxed attitude hadn't helped me find a place to call home yet, as illustrated by my fucked-up decision to join this pack. But even I had my limits and Rob was getting close to pushing me right over the edge. He'd been irritating me for a couple of days now and I'd been trying to justify his sniping as a test of loyalty. But this was more than that now. He was pissing me off, and no one wanted to face a pissed off hellhound, not even a wolf pack alpha.

It usually took a lot for someone to drive me to this point. I had a high tolerance for bullshit, but I didn't this time. I blamed that on my disappointment, which was my own damn fault. The wolf pack hadn't broken any promises to me; they just hadn't lived up to my hopes and expectations.

"No, I cannot," the alpha snapped. He added a growly sound to his words, as if trying to intimidate me and anyone else who might try to question him. "Just do as you're told."

I closed my eyes. I really couldn't do that.

The alpha obviously didn't know shit about hell-hounds, or he'd know he was asking the impossible. I frowned. I'd hoped to stay here at least a year—maybe even a lifetime if everything went to plan—and I hadn't even made it a week. Still, as the only supe here who wasn't a wolf, maybe I should have been happy I'd even made it this long.

A familiar hollowness in my chest ached as the last lingering bit of hope I'd been clinging to burnt to ash.

"That's our territory." The alpha turned back to his devout packmates and pointed aggressively toward the east.

My nose twitched at the odor in the air from the alpha's words. *Partially true, but not quite right.*

My ability to scent lies was helpful, but I wished I understood why he was lying. Not all lies were bad, right? I snorted. Yeah. I couldn't even pretend to believe that. My unyielding honesty had gotten me into trouble almost as much as my ability to scent lies other people said, but I couldn't imagine living any other way.

Even if it meant I was destined to live alone.

"That's our pack house," the alpha continued. *Another half-truth.*

He spoke loudly, in a rallying sort of way, which I guess was one way to get people to feel good about stealing. He sounded more like a con man promoting a Ponzi scheme than a wolf pack alpha. I rubbed my aching head.

A spot behind my left eye started throbbing.

"So anything in that place is ours." *An outright lie.* "It's time for us to go and get it." The alpha cracked his knuckles. "Josh here, he's already led a test run. Went smooth as…Er…" the alpha fumbled over his words like he couldn't remember the idiom. "As slick as bacon grease. That's right. It went as slick as bacon grease to get into the pack house and back out again."

Yeah. Our illustrious alpha certainly had a way with words. I couldn't believe it when the pack hummed in approval. A few licked their lips.

"And Lenny, he's already lined up a buyer from the city. A gnome… or was it a goblin…?" The alpha cut his hand through the air when Lenny tried to step in to explain. Lenny cringed and dropped his gaze.

Truth.

Some of the wolves growled low about the mere idea of working with another supe.

Me? I was wondering if that was who I'd seen Lenny talking to in the woods the first night I'd joined the pack. They'd been in the deepest shadows of the trees, in a spot so dark even my hellhound's eyes couldn't penetrate it, which was strange now that I thought about it. My hellhound didn't usually have trouble seeing into any shadow. Could magic have been interfering with my senses? If it was, I doubted it was just a gnome or goblin Lenny was talking to. Their magics didn't work like that.

What was this pack mixed up in?

The alpha nodded at the discontented wolves. "I know. I know. I'd prefer to work with a wolf too, but this creature is connected. Better than our usual circle. This is special-ized shit. Magic and shit. Our usual wolf connections won't touch the stuff. Idiots, the lot of them, saying no to that kind of money. But we don't need them."

Truth, at least as far as the alpha was concerned.

As I mulled all that over, I fought the instinct to tilt my head to the side like a confused dog. Not that the wolves would notice, because they did it all the time too. But sitting here, surrounded by these people, I didn't want to be anything like them. Also, I had no desire to show deference to this idiot, and exposing my neck to him might suggest that's what I was doing.

"If that place is the pack house, why do we live here?" As soon as the question left my mouth, I knew I should have saved it to ask later, when the alpha wasn't around, but it was out there now.

The alpha and the rest of the wolves turned to look at me, so I gestured around the room as if they didn't understand what I was asking.

I'd always assumed this dilapidated farmhouse was the pack house. Sure, it wasn't much to look at, but it wasn't terribly different from some of the other shifter settlements I'd visited in the past. There was one large building, in this case a two-story farmhouse with this large musty room in the basement, situated in the center of the development. This was where the alpha lived. All the meals and gatherings were held here too.

Scattered haphazardly around the farmhouse like clusters of mismatched dice were much smaller buildings. Although in better shape than the farmhouse, most of those buildings were no bigger than garden sheds. I'd never been in one of them, but I couldn't figure out how those tiny structures could fit beds let alone families.

Then there was the converted garage, which was where I'd been put.

As soon as the alpha had laid eyes on my muscles, he'd decided I'd be a good guard or enforcer and that was where people holding those positions bunked. But I also suspected he didn't want me mingling with the rest of the pack yet. Not until I'd proven myself.

The garage acted like a barracks, although perhaps calling it 'converted' was being too generous. It was a decrepit old two-car garage with no insulation and large vehicle-sized doors that occasionally opened for no apparent reason. Bunkbeds, stacked three high, were crowded in half of the space with only a foot or two maximum between the mattresses. The other half was used as a common room with threadbare sofas and an ancient box television. As soon as I'd seen the place, I'd dreaded the idea of spending a winter in there, even if I was a hellhound and naturally generated a lot of body heat.

And, honestly, I was too damn old to be crawling to the top of a bunkbed, no matter what time of year it was.

I should have left as soon as I'd seen it.

So, if there was another pack house, why the hell weren't we using it instead of squeezing into these too tight and inadequate accommodations?

"Shh…" Peter, the guy sitting beside me, elbowed me and shook his head. I could see he meant it as a friendly warning, but it irritated me. Mine was a serious question. Had I walked into the middle of a territory war? Because that was not what I'd signed up for when I'd come here almost a week ago.

"Is this not the pack house?" I looked the alpha right in the eye.

The alpha growled and narrowed his eyes at me. "You are supposed to listen and do as I tell you. You're the muscle. You aren't here because of your brains. Got it?"

"Yeah. Except you don't get the brawn without answering my questions."

The alpha rushed toward where I was seated and

leaned over me. His growl was menacing; spit dripped from his extended teeth and landed on my jeans. His eyes flashed gold, showing how close to the surface his animal was. The display was meant to intimidate.

Too bad for him it took more than a partially shifted wolf to scare me.

"Is this not the pack house?" I asked again, calm in the face of his aggression. At this point I didn't have anything more to lose since I wasn't staying anyway, but I was curious. I liked having answers.

"Get out." The alpha attempted to backhand me, but I easily ducked and evaded the hit.

The guy didn't have a clue how to fight someone who wasn't frozen in place as they cowered in fear. It would have no doubt been a valuable lesson to show him what happened when he couldn't bully someone into submission, but what would be the point?

I scooped my bag from the floor beside my chair and made my way to the rickety stairs. He snapped at me, but his teeth didn't touch me. Maybe he wasn't so stupid after all.

When I'd packed up my few belongings this morning, I'd done it on a hunch. I'd hoped the day would go differently, but I wasn't surprised it hadn't.

"Hey, you," the alpha shouted at my back as I climbed the creaky stairs. "If you tell anyone about this meeting, you're dead. Got it?"

"Whatever." I waved away the threat.

These wolves needed to get out more. They didn't understand anything about my kind, and that made me think they probably didn't know much about anything other than being a wolf. And truthfully, they weren't very good at being wolves either. A good, strong wolf pack looked out for each other. They were united by loyalty, friendship, and love, not fear, greed, and ignorance.

I sighed again as I pulled my bag up on to my shoulder. At this rate I sounded like an angsty teenager with all this sighing, and I hated it'd come to this.

No one stopped my exit.

When I got outside, I inhaled deeply, drawing in the soothing scents of the pine and aspen forest. The wolf pack was shit but their property was beautiful, even with night cloaking the land. I should have left earlier, before the sun went down, but I'd needed to give the pack one more chance.

I shouldn't have bothered. What a waste of time.

The darkness didn't bother me, but it wouldn't bother the wolves either. This was their territory. They may have let me walk out of the basement, but I knew they'd come after me. I was too much of a liability to let free. They probably thought the idea of chasing me down in their beast form would be a good fun training exercise. Wolves like these tended to think they were superior to every other supe until someone finally came along to show them how wrong they were.

And it looked like that might be my job tonight.

I stretched, cracking my neck to loosen my muscles. I wasn't scared of the fight ahead. I was a hellhound after all. I was built to fight. But I didn't have to like it.

For now, all I had to decide was which way to go. I sniffed the air again. Nothing called to my beast.

Well, the alpha had pointed east. Maybe that was

enough of a sign. I huffed out a breath, disgusted at the sensation of hope I could feel unfurling in my chest again.

When would I learn? It didn't matter which direction I went; I'd only find more of the same. I knew that.

So why hadn't I figured out how to accept that yet? When was I going to learn hellhounds were meant to be alone?

And the real question was: Why did I crave being with others so much if it was impossible?

Chapter Three

ASH

The greenish glow from my truck's dashboard was too bright and distracting. And, almost as irritating, I couldn't figure out how to make the damn thing dimmer. Whoever designed my vehicle obviously thought everyone drove in the city, surrounded by streetlights.

I held my hand over the brightest part of the console to block the light as I squinted into the trees on either side of the empty road. I'd done the same thing every night since Jake shared his vision a week ago and so far neither I nor any of the other searchers had come across a hellhound being hunted by wolves. I wasn't sure if that was a good thing or not. I hoped we hadn't missed them.

Luckily, my boss had been understanding when I'd told him I couldn't work nights this week, but I wasn't going to get away with working only day shifts next week too.

And, who knew? Maybe the vision was for some future

event a month or a year or a decade from now. Then what? How long would we keep up the patrols?

I huffed out a breath and tapped my fingers on the steering wheel. I couldn't worry about that. I had one task tonight. If we didn't find anyone out here in the woods again, figuring out our next step was tomorrow's problem.

Van and Hayden had assigned each volunteer a specific area to patrol, and I was getting insanely bored of the one they'd given to me. Not for the first time I wished my BFF Jeremy was here with me. He could fill silence easier than anyone I knew. There were only two problems with that idea: one, Jeremy lived a couple of hours away, and two, he didn't know anything about supes.

Could I even call him my best friend when he didn't know I was a mage? Then again, was I even a mage if I couldn't work magic anymore?

These were the kinds of questions that chased me up and down this dull stretch of road.

My phone beeped.

I pulled to the side of the road to check my messages. There were two.

MyBestestBFF4ever: When a shifter changes, do they keep the same mass? Like if my dad was a shifter and changed into a housecat, would he be a 200-pound housecat? Because that would be awesome.

Me: ROFLMAO

MyBestestBFF4ever: And what would happen to his beer belly and his bald spot? Would those traits carry through? Imagine it: a gigantic, pot-

bellied housecat with a bald spot. He'd look
like the feline version of Friar Tuck.

Me: I will never look at your dad the same way
again… *laughing emoji*

The other text was just Van checking in again, like he did every fifteen minutes. He was back at the police station, keeping track of everyone, and on standby for the moment someone saw something. I sent back a thumbs up emoji, then got back on the road again.

We'd already been out for a couple of hours, and I was beginning to doubt tonight would be any different from the last few nights. How many nights would we come out here? Sure, I'd volunteered to do this, but I hadn't expected it to be so… lonesome. And the quiet of the nearly moonless night along a monotonous tree-lined road wasn't helping my mood.

I usually kept busy so memories couldn't find me.

I filled my life with people and noise and activities. I worked every shift I could at the Flying Rowan Café, hung out at the Willow Lake Pub more often than some of the town drunks, ate out for both lunch and dinner, and sat through the same movie at the Larch Theatre night after night, even though the ones they showed were already available on Netflix.

And when those things didn't work, I called my mom, my brother, or my best friend—like actually called them, not texted. Just to fill up the quiet. Jeremy and Birch didn't even answer half the time, but I still tried. Which meant I spoke to my mom way more than any other guy my age, but I couldn't stop. I didn't handle being alone well and no amount of therapy was going to change that. Thankfully, my mom was a social creature and hadn't seemed to realize what I was doing. If she had, she'd have insisted I move back home more doggedly than she already did.

Would it be so very bad if I pulled over to the side of the road and scrolled through social media for a bit? Maybe send a few memes or thirty to Jeremy? I couldn't do either of those things while driving, but they'd both distract me for a bit. I frowned. No. I shouldn't. Getting lost in cute cat videos wasn't what I was out here for. Unfortunately.

I chewed on my bottom lip. If we had to come out here another night, maybe I'd download an audio book or something, anything so it wasn't so terribly quiet. That would be perfect, actually. Why hadn't I thought of that six days ago?

I rolled down my window. That should help, right? More noise, more scents, more fresh air sweeping over my skin. If I were a shifter, I'd hear things out there—howls or panting breaths or pounding paws. Hell, even if I was a better mage—an undamaged one—I'd be able to send my magic into the forest and sense for supernatural creatures. But, yeah, that wasn't going to happen either. The familiar ache in my chest flared to life. I rubbed it and the scar tissue absently with the heel of my palm. Then that irritating pressure built up inside me until I let out a little burp.

I groaned.

Why did this always have to happen when I thought about my magic?

The hair on my forearms rose as the air from outside

rolled over me. I knew it wasn't truly cold, not when every single person in Willow Lake was complaining it was too hot at night to sleep, but I shivered anyway. I cranked up the heater.

Yeah, yeah, it was stupid to keep the heater on when I had the windows down and hot air streaming into the cab, but I wasn't about to turn it off. Not even on a hot night like tonight.

Another shiver rolled over me, as if to reinforce the point.

Fuck it. I couldn't do this. I rolled up the window, then reached for the radio. The first station that wasn't just static was playing country music. I could live with that. A lot of the locals listened to it, so I'd gotten to know some of the songs since moving here. The current song had the singer loving how his woman thought his tractor was sexy. Yeah. Country music didn't always make sense to me, but the tune was catchy enough to keep my thoughts from straying.

I tapped the steering wheel absently in time with the song as I scanned the tree line.

A hellhound would be bright, right? I should check to make sure. I slowed the truck and scanned the texts, just like I had twenty minutes ago. And ten times the night before. And fifty times the night before that. I know. I probably shouldn't look at my phone while driving but needs must and all that. I scrolled through the messages until I found the text I was looking for, and, yeah, the hellhound would be lit up like a bonfire. Van had said as much. I mean, I knew that, but the dark and the quiet of the night were messing with me, making me question things. Even really obvious things.

Something flashed in the darkness to the left, like lightning except the sky was clear.

I eased down on the brakes. Was I seeing things?

No. There it was again. I leaned forward and stared into the trees. Yes. That was the creature. The hellhound. Which meant…

A series of angry howls rose in a chorus from deeper in the woods, audible even over the music, the engine, and the hum of the heater. Fear skittered down my spine. This fear, it was different from the fear I'd experienced when my magic had been attacked, maybe because the part of my brain I'd inherited from some long-ago ancestor recognized the threat in those howls, making my survival instincts kick in.

Whereas when my magic had been threatened, I hadn't known any fear until it was too late. My hind brain hadn't registered the threat because witches weren't supposed to harm one another. The attack on my magic shouldn't have happened.

I rubbed my chest again, this time to calm the panic seizing my heart.

Screams of *run, run, run* and *danger, danger, danger* and *oh fuck* roared through my head. My every instinct begged me to leave the beasts in the trees far, far behind.

Except I couldn't leave without the hellhound. That was the whole point of being out here.

The hairs on the back of my neck stood on end as I forced the truck to slow even more. I was nearly at the place where, based on their trajectory, I expected the hellhound to break free of the trees. I swiped the back of my hand over my mouth. The ball of fiery light around the creature grew brighter and bigger the nearer it came.

Shit. The thing was huge.

Then they burst onto the road. I slammed on the brakes and fumbled to open my door. I managed to get it open, then I leaned out the door with one hand on the steering wheel and one foot on the brake. No way was I stepping out of the cab. I wasn't putting the truck in Park either.

I refused to leave the safety of my only means of escape.

"Get in," I shouted. I sent my free hand flailing through the air in what was supposed to be a come here motion but probably made me look like I was having a seizure. "Hurry. Get in."

The wolves, who were too damn close for my comfort, cried out, warning me away, but the hellhound merely swung their head to look at me. The creature's eyes shone in the dark like glowing embers. Golden fire flowed over their massive back, licking wildly along their glistening, midnight black fur. A blaze of luminous oranges and reds curled around their enormous black claws, which protruded from even larger black paws. I gulped. When the beast snorted in response, flames erupted from their mouth and nostrils in a glow of white-blue. Even from this distance I could feel the blast of heat.

"Please. They're coming." I felt breathless. If I hyper-ventilated and passed out…

It was probably better not to think about what would happen.

Already the shadows under the trees were undulating

with movement. The wolves were almost upon us. Fuck it. If the hellhound didn't want help, I wasn't sticking around to die with them. I fell back into the driver's seat and slammed my door closed.

In a blur of movement, the hellhound shifted into a muscular titan of a man dressed in faded jeans and a tight black T-shirt. His short brown hair had a bit of a wave to it that seemed at odds with the sharp angles of his face. The duffle bag he'd been carrying in his mouth dropped and he caught it in his big meaty hand before it hit the ground.

The guy's wariness was obvious when he didn't immediately jump inside the truck. But really, how could I be considered a worse threat than the bloodthirsty mob tracking him through the hills? I'm not ashamed of my slim body, but the guy had to have at least fifty pounds on me, easy. It was pretty obvious I wasn't a threat to him. He took his sweet ass time as he approached the truck slowly.

"Come on, come on, come on," I muttered, as I squinted at the trees again.

A host of frenzied eyes glinted back at me under the glow of my headlights. Shitty shit shit.

I yanked on my miniscule well of magic and threw a curtain of light and flames across the ditch. Well, it was only an illusion, but it'd buy us a few minutes. Maybe. Hopefully.

Shifted werewolves were more animal than human, or so I'd heard. I was banking on that now. Praying they'd be leery of getting too close to what appeared to be a deadly wildfire. At least until they figured out my light show wasn't a threat.

The hellhound barely spared my diversion a glance as he opened the passenger door.

"You here because of the alpha?"

"Just get in." My tight and sweaty grip slipped over the smooth steering wheel.

"Did the alpha send you?"

"You mean Robbie? That's where you were, right? In that pack in the hills? If that's who you mean, then no. I'm here to save your ass. But if you want to stick around here, I can't stop you."

The hellhound made a big production of inhaling deeply. He nodded, as if satisfied with whatever he scented. The wolves were breaking through my flimsy illusion now—looking more like a bunch of circus animals jumping through fire rings than a deadly pack hunting for blood.

"If you're coming, get the fuck in," I snapped, not even looking at the guy now. I was too transfixed on wolf after wolf after wolf emerging from the trees. My breath tore from my lungs in tight short bursts. "I swear to fuck if you don't move it in the next—"

The stranger dove inside. Thank fuck. The door hadn't even shut when I gunned it.

Chapter Four

DILLON

I yanked my legs inside the cab of the truck and righted myself in the seat. Then I quickly shoved my bag down by my feet and grabbed the door to slam it shut. Holy hell it was hot in here, even by my standards. Did he seriously have the heater blasting in this weather?

I eyed the stranger.

He was decidedly handsome with his messy dark hair and green eyes so pale they almost looked gray. Sure, it was dark inside the cab of his truck, but I could see him clearly when I let my hellhound's flames enter my eyes. The guy had a bit of a scruff over his jaw and pale pink lips that looked invitingly soft. That pink matched the color of his fluffy sweater, which drew my attention back to his mouth again. Not that I was going to kiss him or anything. But today had been spectacularly shitty, and I'd learned a long time ago it was good to stop and appreciate beauty when I saw it.

Maybe being saved by a handsome man was a sign that my luck was improving.

Yeah. Right.

I was never that lucky.

"Hi there," my would-be rescuer said. He sounded out of breath and his heart was beating faster than a humming-bird's wings. An anxious laugh shot out of his mouth. "You need a lift into town?"

He forced a smile, and I knew he was trying to joke about the situation. When I didn't laugh, his gaze darted to me. He rolled his hands over his steering wheel.

"Is that okay? Going to town, I mean? Because that's the plan."

I inhaled again. I still didn't sense any deceit and I hoped that meant I could trust him. When I'd first seen the guy while in my hellhound form, the glow of his magic had eclipsed everything else. Power pulsed around him. He was more of a threat than all those pups chasing me through the woods just now.

"Witch?"

The guy lifted his shoulder in a stiff half-shrug. "We usually call ourselves mages, but witch works too."

"Who sent you here if it wasn't the alpha?"

"That asshole isn't my alpha and his merry band of fuckwits aren't my pack. I already said I'm not here because of him." He paused and squished up his nose. "Or I guess maybe I am because they were chasing you. The oracle, who we didn't know was an oracle, gave us the message they were after you. But I'm not here because I personally know that sorry excuse for an alpha or those wolves. Never met them. They were gone when I moved here. Only seen them from a distance, you know? Well, I guess you don't. You're not from here, are you? I would have remembered you..." The guy's cheeks darkened. "Spells and curses, why am I talking so much? Why were they chasing you anyway?"

His nervous babbling was kind of cute. Actually, the witch as a whole was cute. And he hadn't spoken any lies yet. So that also helped increase his adorableness by a factor of ten.

"I stayed there for a bit. They kicked me out today," I said, figuring I could offer the witch a bit of information since he had helped me out. Not that I'd needed help. I would have figured something out. But this was a hell of a lot easier.

The witch nodded.

I leaned back in the seat and concentrated on cooling down, which wasn't easy when the temperature in the cab of the truck rivaled the inside of an active volcano. As a hellhound, I never minded heat, but I needed control right now, which meant I needed to cool the flames still churning through me. My hellhound's fire always heated my blood and made me feel volatile. Flames danced under the surface of my skin, still fighting to be free, eager to char the bastards who had decided to hunt me down through the woods.

"You alone?" The witch glanced in his mirrors. The wolves wouldn't have been able to keep up with the truck, but the guy might not know that. Different kinds of supes didn't often interact with one another.

"Yes."

"Like I said, we're going back to town. Hope that's okay. It's safer than out here anyway."

"So there is a town? I wasn't sure," I said, glancing out the window at the dense woods along the side of the road. "I was hoping to find a motel."

"Willow Lake isn't much, but we like it. And I'm sure there are some vacancies at the motel or the inn." The guy's shoulder relaxed a touch, and the truck slowed as his fears eased.

I doubted he'd have let down his guard so quickly if he could still hear the wolves baying in the night like I could. Witches tended to have weak senses, not much better than regular humans. I wasn't sure if it was cruel or a blessing that the Eternal Magic had given the weaker species such dull senses.

"Name's Ash, by the way. Ash Avery," the witch said.

"Dillon Emerson."

Another engine roared through the quiet. It was loud and coming fast. Ash didn't react until headlights rounded the bend in the road behind us.

"Shit." Ash adjusted the rearview mirror. "Think that's them?"

"Probably."

Our truck fishtailed on the loose gravel as Ash floored the gas again. Pebbles pinged off the undercarriage.

"Crap. Okay," Ash said.

"How far to town?" I grabbed the oh shit handle as the truck careened down the road.

"Couple of miles."

That was doable. As long as Ash managed to keep us ahead of the others and out of the ditch, we should be fine.

"The wolves up in the hills are assholes, but I've never heard of them hunting people down. Or do they do this all the time and no one's ever found the bodies?" Ash paled at the idea.

"I know something the alpha doesn't want me to tell anyone else. That's why they're after me," I said. It was weird how much I wanted to ease the little witch's worry. I couldn't imagine Ash sleeping at night if he thought the hills were full of werewolf serial killers.

Ash grunted and clenched his fingers around the steering wheel as he guided us around another bend. As soon as we survived the turn, the witch peeled his fingers off the wheel and fished for something in his pocket. He pulled out a phone. He fumbled with it for a second, unlocking it, then tossed it to me.

"Look for Van Clark in my contact list. Call him and tell him what's going on."

I didn't want to take my eyes off the other truck that long—particularly when the damn thing was getting closer—but having backup might be a good thing.

The call was answered on the first ring.

"*Ash? Did you find him?* "

"Hey. This isn't Ash. He told me to tell you we're being followed—"

"Chased." Ash shouted, presumably so the guy on the other end of the call could hear. "Not followed, chased. By a truck. Along the old Spruce Road."

The guy on the phone—Van, presumably—swore.

"Did you hear all that?" I asked.

"*Yeah… I'm coming.*"

Our pursuers rammed into our bumper. The phone flew

from my hand, landed on the floorboards, then tumbled out of sight beneath the seat. The truck skidded. Ash cursed.

"Are they trying to kill us?" Ash shouted.

I laughed. "Yeah. Pretty sure they are."

"I'll haunt those fuckers and make their lives miserable." Ash laughed then too. It sounded desperate and not at all happy.

Well, that thought sobered me up. I mean, I wasn't concerned about myself. I was hard to kill, but a witch was more fragile. Sure, this guy was powerful, but a witch's body wasn't built to withstand physical trauma and fights like a shifter. A strange pain cut through my chest at the idea of this witch being injured because of me, because of the trouble I brought, however unintentionally. I'd barely even met the guy, but I didn't want to see him harmed.

"Shit, I wasn't thinking. I shouldn't have gotten in—"

"Shut the fuck up," Ash growled. It was a surprisingly menacing sound coming from a witch. "I'm concentrating and don't need your sorry ass apologies when we both know this is on that dumbass wannabe alpha."

I bit back a grin at the witch's command, I'd always had a thing for the feisty ones. Yeah. Like now was the time to think with my dick. I eyed our tail. Ash had pulled ahead by a few feet, but the others were gaining on us again. I twisted and peered into the back seat. If I crawled back there, I could fit through the window closest to the other vehicle. Probably. If I jumped onto it, I could… do what? I wasn't sure. But it'd at least get the attention off Ash.

"Don't you fucking dare," Ash shouted when I started to crawl into the back seat.

Then over the cacophony of country music, revving engines, and gravel clunking against the undercarriage was the shrill whine of a siren.

"We're almost there and I can hear sirens," Ash said.

Apparently, the wolves in the other vehicle could hear the sirens too because suddenly they dropped their pursuit. Then they spun a one-eighty and raced back down the road.

Ash didn't slow. We flew past the *Town of Willow Lake* welcome sign. An unexpected jumble of unfamiliar magic enveloped me. Two cop cars with lights flashing and sirens blaring shot past us in pursuit of the wolf pack's vehicle. Another car threw a quick U-turn and followed us.

"Hey," I said, "we made it. You can stop now."

When Ash didn't respond, I risked touching him to jolt him out of his panicked flight through town. The witch blinked, like he was finally aware of his surroundings.

"Shit," Ash muttered, but he pulled the vehicle over and stopped. He was still white knuckling the steering wheel when the cop exited his vehicle and walked alongside the driver's side.

"Ash?" the cop said as he tapped on the window. "You okay?"

Ash's eyes flashed with light as his magic flared. Then he flew into action. He threw the vehicle into Park, turned off the ignition and wrenched open the door to glare at the cop. "No. No, Van, I'm not okay. Those bastards tried to kill us. They rammed my truck. If they dented it, I swear…"

"You're okay." Van lifted his hands in a placating way and stepped closer to Ash.

It could be to console or comfort him, but what if it wasn't? I had decided a few miles back I'd keep the little witch safe. That decision didn't end because the wolves had been chased away. My instincts to *protect, protect, protect* roared to life. This Van guy needed to back up and get the hell away from Ash. Except Ash wasn't shying away from the guy.

Were these two lovers? I growled. The sound was deep and angry, showing how close I was to my shift. My hellhound side geared up to pounce, ready to annihilate the threat to what was mine.

Mine? Oh, no. That wasn't right. What was I thinking? I didn't know this witch. I couldn't just claim people. It wasn't done. I shook my head. *Not cool, beast, not cool. It's been a long time since our kind moved out of caves.*

Then the intruder's smoky scent hit me, and my beast froze.

"What the—?"

Van's eyes snapped to mine. Fire blazed in his irises. Fire. Like a hellhound's fire. Confirming what I'd already scented. My jaw dropped.

"Calm down, hellhound," Van said. "We're here to help you."

It looked like I wasn't the only hellhound left in the world after all.

Chapter Five

DILLON

"Start from the beginning," Van said as he spun his pen between his fingers. His notebook was open in front of him. I took it as a good sign we were in a meeting room at the police station instead of an interrogation room. Even better, Ash had been allowed to stay with me.

I didn't know why I wanted to keep the witch close, but I did.

Instead of talking, I grabbed another piece of extra spicy beef jerky from the bag he'd given me to replenish my magic after my shift and my race through the woods. I gave it to Ash, since he'd used magic tonight too, then took a piece for myself.

I leaned back in my chair and eyed the other hellhound as I chewed. I was getting tired of going over all this, so he had to be tired of it too. Besides, I had my own fair share of questions, but Van wasn't interested in entertaining any of those until he was satisfied with my answers.

I doubted he was trying to be cruel, but I hadn't seen another hellhound in… well, a long, long time, and I wanted to know more. Did other hellhounds live here? If they didn't, where were they? Did hellhounds typically abandon their young?

And then there was Willow Lake. Was the bizarre blend of energies in the air a product of the so-called supernatural paradise? I'd never felt anything like it. It was too unusual to be entirely comfortable, but maybe it'd grow on me since I suspected this was the place I'd been looking for when I'd first traveled this way. Once again, the persistent sliver of hope in my chest tried to expand. I pushed it down and forced my attention back to Van's question.

I opened my mouth to tell my story. Again. For the fourth time. The sooner Van got the answers he was looking for, the sooner I'd get mine.

"Where is he?" The loud male voice rose over the din of muted conversations outside of the room and drew all our attention. "Don't make me sniff him out. There. He's in there, isn't he? Step aside, Dot. I don't want to have to use my alpha will on you."

When Van's lips twitched into a near smile and Ash's breath hitched, I sat up and braced myself. The door burst open. My blood heated as my hellhound rose in me. Neither Van nor Ash's reactions suggested the newcomer was a threat, but I wasn't ready to trust anyone here. Not yet.

Well, except maybe the witch, for reasons I couldn't explain.

A man with messy light brown hair pushed past the

wide-eyed deer shifter who'd been standing outside the room. The intruder's square jaw was tight with anger, then his eyes flashed, showing his wolf. His jeans were stained with who knew what and he wore a T-shirt with a faded band logo on the front. I recognized it as a human band, but I couldn't remember what kind of music they played.

"What's going on? Why do you have Dot listening at the door?"

Van frowned and glanced toward the deer shifter, who scurried away. He got up and shut the door. "She shouldn't have been."

"Alpha," Ash said in deference, tilting his head to the side to bare his throat to the newcomer. And wasn't that an odd thing for a mage to do?

Was this another pack? In my experience, wolf packs didn't usually have territories so close together. And I'd never seen one accept mages. I eyed the new arrival. He looked a bit familiar, but I was sure I'd never met the guy before. I inhaled deeply and froze.

A low growl rumbled along the back of my throat.

Underneath the stink of motor oil was the scent I thought I'd left behind earlier today, because there was no doubt this guy was kin to the asshole alpha in the woods. Now that I knew that, the familiar shape of his face was obvious.

"Easy there," Van said to me.

Didn't he know who this guy was?

Van met my eyes with his steady, calm gaze. It was clear the other hellhound trusted the newcomer.

I inhaled again to confirm my suspicions about the wolf. The scent connection was weak. Rob and this guy obviously didn't spend any time together. That was… intriguing. Fine. I could wait a few minutes and see what would happen. But if I caught the guy in any lies, nothing would stop me from grabbing Ash and making a run for the door.

"Hello, Hayden," Van said. "I was wondering when you'd show up."

The wolf glared at the hellhound. "You should have called me the minute they got into town."

Van rolled his shoulders. "I sent a group text. Not my problem if you don't check your messages. Besides, I work for the Town and the Supernatural Council, not you personally."

The alpha growled, but his stance changed subtly, like he suddenly remembered he wasn't the one in charge. It was strange for an alpha to back down like that. Hayden grabbed the chair beside Van, swung it around and then sat on it with the back against his chest. The air around him smelled of wolf and the grungy corner of a mechanic's shop.

"Before we continue, tell Dillon that you aren't working with Robbie so he doesn't combust."

Hayden narrowed his eyes at me. His nostrils flared as he inhaled. "So this is the hellhound?"

Van nodded.

"I am not working with Robbie," Hayden said evenly.

Truth.

"You mean Rob, right? The alpha of the pack?"

"Yeah," Van said. "He'll always be Robbie to me, and probably Hayden too since the little shit is Hayden's brother. He left here to start his own pack several years ago, but I expect most of us here would have a hell of a time thinking of him as an alpha. Good enough? That clear things up?"

I nodded. I'd accept Hayden in here for now. I wouldn't be using the name Robbie, though. It made the belligerent asshole alpha sound like he should be six years old and running around with a dirty T-shirt and scuffed knees.

"Okay. Good. Now, Dillon here was just going to tell us what happened."

"I don't know why we have to do this again." I rolled my eyes. "You know I'm not lying."

Hellhounds couldn't tell a lie. They could smell lies in the air. They could see them on someone's face. But they couldn't tell one themselves. Based on a lifetime of unfortunate experiences with other supes, I knew that was a little-known fact. And, ironically, when I, one of the world's last hellhounds—though earlier today I would have said I *was* the last—tried to explain my hellhound nature to people, they always thought I was lying. But Van would know about the lying thing, since he was a hellhound too. So, why was he being like this?

"I know that," Van acknowledged with a slight nod. "But we need details, and you don't seem great at giving those."

He wanted details. Fine. I would dig out my mental fucking thesaurus and dump details all over the man.

"A couple of weeks ago, on a windy Wednesday morning, I overheard two supes—a small female faun and a larger male centaur—talking at a coffee shop in the city. I believe they were coworkers. I don't remember the name of the place. It was on Water Street, in an old converted warehouse. The cappuccino was decent. The biscotti had almonds and chocolate—"

Ash covered his mouth to hide his snort of laughter. Everyone at the table heard it.

Van rolled his eyes. "Don't be an ass. None of us has time for that."

"You asked for details…"

"How about you stick to *pertinent* details?"

"Fine." I nodded. "They said Willow Lake was a good place for supes of all kinds. The faun had vacationed here recently, or something. Anyway, I was looking for a change and thought I'd check it out. So I signed into Supenet and found the local pack. The pack name wasn't listed, but the address was. Thought that was as good a place as any to start."

Hayden frowned and crossed his arms over his chest.

"I got there about a week back. The alpha, Rob, was a bit of a jerk, but the rest of the pack was okay. No one was overly welcoming, but it usually takes people time to get used to having a hellhound around, so I wasn't worried." I rubbed my neck. "But as the days passed, nothing was improving, and I wasn't seeing any sign of what the supes at the coffee shop were talking about. The pack was full of wolf shifters and no one else. I'm surprised the pack even took me in, but the alpha seemed happy enough to have a hellhound around. He kept going on and on about how we're genetic cousins and that made me acceptable. I think he thought I was desperate enough for a pack that I'd be an obedient enforcer for him. Kept talking about how big I was, like my muscles were all I was good for. Asked me to donate my car to the pack as dues. The hatchback was a shitty thing I'd picked up for a couple hundred, so I figured he could have it."

I didn't mention I hadn't minded giving up the car if it meant finding a place to stay. A home. The men in this room didn't need to know that. There'd been a few times in my life when I'd settled in one place for a few decades before moving on, but I'd always known I'd leave. Nothing had ever felt permanent or stable. Nothing'd ever felt right.

Hell, for most of the last century, I hadn't even managed to stay that long. Something always drove me on. Constantly searching. Constantly dreaming that maybe the next place would be *the place*. They didn't need to hear Rob was right about how fucking desperate I was to find some place to put down roots. Hell, this time I hadn't even lasted a week because even desperation couldn't override my inherent sense of right and wrong.

Van snorted. "I could see him being thrilled, imagining he had a hellhound willing to blindly follow his orders. Robbie never was very smart."

"Right? There was no way," I agreed, grinning at Van. It was such a novelty to have someone who understood what being a hellhound was like. I could no more follow an order without knowing my actions were just and morally right than I could stop fire from covering my body when I was in my shifted form. "Besides I am too damn old to rough it like they were. Sure, there was a roof over my head, but sleeping on a bunk bed in a drafty, uninsulated garage with a bunch of unkempt wolves is hardly my dream life. So I was already thinking of moving on when Rob called a pack meeting today."

Hayden listened to me with an intensity that almost had me squirming, except I was a hellhound, and we didn't let anyone intimidate us.

"I want to know more about the layout of the pack lands, but we can go over that later." Van glanced at Hayden. "Do you think Robbie was testing Dillon? Or trying to feed us wrong information through him?"

"Or he's forgotten about hellhounds and how they can sense lies. Either that, or he never believed it to begin with." Hayden shrugged. "Remember? He never used to attend meetings with you."

"True," Van said.

"That's not the important thing, though," Hayden said, looking squarely at me. His alpha power, which was a hell of a lot more potent than Rob's had ever been, rolled out over us. Ash shivered at my side. "What happened out there? Why did you run? Why were they chasing you?"

"Right," Van said. "Let's talk about the pack meeting again. Tell us everything you remember."

I finished the water Van had given me when we'd first arrived and gathered my thoughts. As soon as I set the glass down, Ash filled it again. I nodded my thanks. It was nice to have the mage there. I couldn't explain why, but knowing the guy was safe helped me focus.

"Rob started off by having everyone howl, getting their blood pumping and the adrenaline flowing. Then he rambled on about Willow Lake. Like how they didn't live there, but it was still pack territory. Which I have to say was confusing, because, although they weren't listed in

Supenet under a pack name, they'd been calling themselves the Willow Lake Pack since I arrived."

A faint growl rumbled through the room.

"The Willow Lake Pack… Of course, he did." Hayden shook his head and scowled. "That's a damn lie. Their pack name is Red Hills Pack, the Willow Lake Pack doesn't exist anymore. Damn it. I bet they started using it because they've shafted too many people too many times and no one will work with them now. All they'll end up doing is ruining the Willow Lake name too."

My nose twitched. Interesting. Hayden was telling the truth, at least as he understood it.

"Well," I said, "some part of Rob thinks he's right because it scented as a partial truth. Then he started talking about the pack house, and it was obvious he wasn't talking about the crappy old two-story farmhouse we were meeting in." I closed my eyes, trying to remember exactly how the rest of the meeting went. "So then he says everything in the pack house is theirs and they'd go and get it under the new moon."

Van cleared his throat, and I opened my eyes.

"Did he believe what he was saying?"

I rocked my hand side to side. "Not the part about the stuff being theirs, but everything else, yeah."

Van looked at Hayden who was grinding his teeth now. "That's a problem."

"Do you know specifically what he wants?" Hayden skewered me with his eyes.

Before I could answer, a knock came at the door.

"What?" Van bellowed.

The timid looking deer shifter opened the door and peeked inside.

"Uh, sir? There is someone here, saying they want to give a statement. Something about seeing something they want to report?"

"Who is it?"

"Simon Rivers."

As soon as she said the name, Van waved her away.

"Take his statement. If it looks important, we'll talk about it later. And don't interrupt us again unless someone's life is in danger. Got it?"

"Yes, sir." She closed the door quietly.

"You're never that abrupt with people, particularly employees. What's going on?" Hayden had leaned close to Van, dropping his voice so it was barely a whisper. I shifted my hearing enough to listen. Sue me. I wanted to know what was going in case I needed to act.

"It's like she's forgotten all her training lately. Listening at the door. Asking about things she should know, like whether or not to take someone's damned statement." Van kept his voice just as quiet. He shook his head. "I'll deal with it. Later."

They pulled apart and turned their attention back to me.

"Well?" Hayden prompted. "What does he want? What did Robbie say they were after?"

"He said Lenny had lined up a buyer. Some goblin or gnome from the city. He couldn't remember which. Someone who'd be able to sell magical items. The wolves weren't happy about working with a supe who wasn't a wolf, but Rob said their usual fence wouldn't touch magical artifacts. All that was true, at least as far as Rob was concerned. But Rob figured the money was too good to pass up and was willing to work with the new buyer regardless of their species. Oh, and he said something about already testing out how they were going to steal things. Something like that." My cheeks heated. "Sorry, I'd forgotten about that before."

"Testing out?" Van's hand clenched around his pen. "What does that mean?"

"He didn't go into details, but I got the sense they'd done a trial run."

Van and Hayden both growled. Then Van jumped out of his seat and wrenched open the door to the meeting room. "Dot, get over here."

The same deer shifter trotted over to her boss.

"You finished with that statement?"

She shook her head.

Van frowned. "Get his information so you can take his statement later. I need you to get over to the inn and check on Jake. Make sure he's okay."

The police station was small, but I was surprised they didn't have at least one other officer to help out. There were at least two other people in the office: one alligator shifter at the front desk and a human. Did the human deputy not know about supes? That'd be damn awkward when everyone else in the office was one.

Sensing the gap in the small police force made me want to jump up and get to work. I'd always been drawn to the idea of law enforcement, even becoming a cop for a short while back in the mid-1800s, but I hadn't committed to a profession like that recently because it would tie me to one location, and I'd never found a place I wanted to stay. I wasn't sure Willow Lake would be that place either, but I couldn't help but wonder *what if*?

Dot's light brown eyes widened. "Did something happen?"

"Just do it, Dot. Call me as soon as you talk to him."

Before the deer shifter had even turned away, Van had shut the door in her face and returned to his seat at the table. He looked at Hayden, whose face had started to contort into his wolf's features.

"I'm sure he's fine." Van clapped his hand on to the wolf's shoulder. "Robbie wouldn't want anyone to suspect they'd been there. It'd be too risky to hurt Jake."

Hayden wiped his hand over his face. Slowly, he got control over his wolf.

"We'll head over there after this and talk to Jake about what might be missing."

Hayden nodded at Van, sucking a deep breath. "Jodi is still away?"

"Yes. It's a pain in the ass that all this is happening while we're short staffed."

Hayden grunted, but he seemed calmer now. He turned his eyes back on me. "Anything else?"

"Not much, honestly." I shrugged. "I started asking questions Rob didn't want to answer and he kicked me out." I leaned forward and looked at Van. "How was that for details?"

"Better." Faint praise from the hellhound cop. At least his lips twitched and almost formed a smile.

"Robbie always was a greedy shit." Hayden pushed his fingers through his hair.

"So," I said, "he wouldn't answer, but I still want to know. Is there a pack house here?"

Hayden grimaced. "Not for a long time. Willow Lake doesn't have a pack."

I tilted my head. I had so many questions: like if there wasn't a pack, why did Ash address this wolf as alpha? And how did Hayden ooze alpha energy if he didn't have a pack? Ash leaned over, distracting me all to hell. A zing of energy whipped up my arm when the little mage in the fuzzy pink sweater patted my hand.

"The old pack house was converted into an inn about a decade or more ago," Ash whispered to me, as if sensing the direction of my thoughts. "It was before I moved here, so I'm not sure exactly how long ago."

"So, they want to steal from the Willow Lake Inn under the new moon." Van frowned and tapped his pen against his notebook. "As a plan, it isn't a bad one, I suppose. Most supes are weaker under the new moon. It'd reduce the risk. The new moon would give them a bit of cover. And Ulric's grandkid wouldn't even know what to do if a bunch of wolves showed up in the middle of the night. Jake's a bit naive, even for a human—or an oracle, I guess —but I'm pretty sure he'd notice a bunch of werewolves ripping through the place."

Hayden's eyes flashed golden, showing his wolf. "I'll get Sally and Alice to figure out a way to get him out of there for a couple of nights. Hopefully one night is all it'll take to stop these guys and make them regret setting their eyes on the inn, but we should plan for more just in case. We need to organize a patrol too."

For not being the alpha of the local pack, Hayden

seemed to have just stepped in to take charge. There was a story there, I was sure of it.

"They'll be expecting it," I said. "They'll know I'm here. They'll know it's a possibility I'll have told someone."

"Yeah." Van's eyes blazed with his hellhound's magic for a moment. Then he grinned wickedly, his teeth elongating slightly. "And the bastards still won't be prepared for us."

Chapter Six

ASH

I couldn't believe I'd actually asked a stranger back to my place…

And that Dillon had actually said yes…

Or that this was actually happening.

The only people I'd invited into this apartment were my mom, my brother Birch, and my best friend Jeremy. No one else. Ever.

But I found him on the side of the road and apparently some part of me decided he was mine.

As I slid the key into the lock on my apartment door with one hand, I tried to surreptitiously wipe my other sweaty hand on my T-shirt. I wished the sweat was from feeling too hot, but it wasn't. This sweat was entirely from nerves.

Every part of me had rebelled at the idea of dropping Dillon off at a motel when we'd left the police station. As awkward as it was to admit, I hadn't wanted to let him out of my sight. I didn't understand my reaction to him, but I was following my instincts on this, even if they'd betrayed me in the past.

With it being so late, the apartment building was quiet. My neighbors were probably all in bed by now, and usually I would be too. It was easier to find distractions in the daylight, so I often got up early. That meant I didn't stay up late. But, tonight, I wasn't eager to go to sleep. Suddenly, I was happy I didn't have to work tomorrow, which was an unusual feeling too. I could thank my hell-hound guest for that.

Dillon followed me inside without comment. I turned the lock on the doorhandle but didn't bother with the dead-bolt. That seemed overkill… like I was trying to lock him in or something. He dropped his duffle bag inside the door, then silently prowled after me as I showed him the place. The tour lasted all of five seconds. My one-bedroom apart-ment was on the petite side.

"So," I said.

My gaze darted around the living room, skittered over Dillon, who seemed larger than life in my tiny home, then flitted to the dark TV screen on the wall before going back to Dillon. Now what? A new wave of nerves rushed through me, making my hands tremble.

I knew what I wanted, but was it too soon? Did Dillon even want me too?

I swear I never used to be this awkward, but it'd been a long time since I'd invited an attractive man into my home. This awkwardness was yet another unwanted gift from my psychopathic ex. I rubbed my chest, tracing those too familiar scars under the layers of my clothes. I jerked my hand away. Nope. Didn't want to think about that tonight.

"So," Dillon echoed.

"You thirsty? Hungry? Did you get enough to replenish your magic? Does beef jerky work for hell-hounds? I know it works for wolves, but you aren't a wolf. Well, I mean I guess it must because that's what Van gave you, and as a hellhound he'd know. But, if it wasn't enough, I could make you something. Anything. I mean I don't eat at home a lot—or ever, really—but I try to keep the basics, just in case. Spaghetti maybe? Or tacos? Canned soup? I swear I can cook. You might not think that by what I just listed, but I work as a cook at one of the local restaurants. People seem to like what I make well enough, I think." Damn it, I was rambling again. I clamped my mouth shut.

"It was the spice more than the beef that helped me with my magic. And, no, I'm not hungry."

"Interesting. Spicy foods are good for me too or something cooked over a fire. Either of those things. But if it is both, my magic…" I swallowed down what I was going to say, because my magic didn't really do anything these days. I could eat all the fire roasted meals in the world, and I'd still never feel as good as I used to. "As a kid, I went through a phase where I insisted only marshmallows toasted on a bonfire worked for me. My mom is an air mage, so she didn't know any better and let me get away with it."

"So, you need to eat," he concluded from my rambling.

I waved away his concern. "No. I'm good. The jerky was fine to replenish what I spent. Seriously."

I wiped my palms on my jeans again before I realized what I was doing. Damn it. I was a big ball of fidget. There was no way Dillon hadn't picked up on how anxious I was. Although it wasn't like a hellhound wouldn't know by my scent alone that I was seventy percent nervous, and thirty percent turned on. Shifters definitely had the advantage there. If I were a shifter, would I scent arousal on him too? I would give anything right now to know what he was thinking.

"Uh… want to watch something on TV? I have a lot of channels. Like not just cable, but apps too. Like so many apps." I didn't like being at home, but on those rare occasions I was stuck here, I usually had the TV on to fill the silence.

The big man shook his head, not even glancing toward the TV. "Thank you for this."

Although he spoke quietly, his deep, rumbly voice amped up my arousal. It was weird how my whole body was hyper aware of the guy. His voice made my scalp tingle and my toes curl. Was that weird? Probably. Like, how could a tingling scalp be a good thing? But I wasn't sure I cared right now. Not with the sexy hellhound looking at me like he was ready to strip me and lick me all over. But, holy Magic, my damn dick had been hard for hours now, ever since I'd met him, and the deep seductive tone of his voice had just made it so much worse.

Dillon's mouth twitched. Had he scented my spike in arousal? Did it happen that fast? Apparently so. Well then, wasn't that awkward? I swallowed hard.

"I know I should have insisted on staying at a motel, but I was happy you offered," Dillon said.

"It's all good." I forced myself to look at Dillon, whose gaze was bright with his beast's internal hell fire. Why was that so freaking sexy? Ever since we'd walked into my place, his eyes had been covered in flames. His dark brown eyes were pretty too, but with the flames? Holy magic. That just did something to me.

"Good." Dillon stepped closer. His body heat warmed me, and he wasn't even touching me. His body temperature must run unusually hot. It felt delicious. How weird would it be if I just latched onto him like a parasite and sucked up his heat? "I'm a hellhound. I like truth, so I'm going to lay it all out there." He paused for a moment, giving me the chance to protest if I didn't want to hear what he was about to say. I kept my mouth shut. My heart raced with anticipation. "I'm attracted to you, Ash. And I think you're attracted to me too."

I gulped but managed to nod. Dillon stepped closer again until I had to tilt my head back to keep looking into his fiery eyes. I'd known from the very beginning the hellhound was a big guy, but now, standing so close together, our size difference was even more obvious. He had to have at least six or eight inches on me. And, fuck, it was perfect. I'd always been drawn to the large muscular types, and Dillon was a mountain of a man. It didn't hurt that he was hot as fuck with those firm lips that looked like they'd give the best kisses in the world. And don't even get me started on his chiseled jawline. He was absolutely, one hundred percent my type.

Slowly, as if to let me have the chance to stop this,

Dillon lifted his huge hand to bridge the small gap between our bodies. No way was I stopping him. I wanted this. Wanted him. And that was such a novelty.

My reaction to Dillon had happened so fast... It was crazy. The smart thing would be to slow things down, but every part of me rejected that idea.

I hadn't really wanted anyone in so long, I'd begun to wonder if more than my magic had been damaged by my past mistakes. But I didn't have to wonder about that anymore. Every part of me was surging to life.

Tonight, I wanted nothing more than to revel in this man and this moment.

I didn't want to think about the future. Or the past.

Maybe this was just some life-affirming reaction to being chased down the road by the damn wolves, but I wanted to grab on to this man tonight. I wanted to experience joy and pleasure and the wonder of having a bone melting orgasm with another person. Dillon wouldn't disappoint, I knew that like I knew my own name.

I was already panting when Dillon's massive hand slid around my neck and cupped the back of my head. I hummed at how warm and good it felt. Then I lurched forward, throwing my body against the hard mass of Dillon's muscled one. The hellhound didn't even sway under the force of the impact.

"Want you," I whispered. I eagerly rubbed against his hot body—and yes, he was both literally and figuratively hot.

Then Dillon's mouth met mine in a crush of lips, the clack of teeth, and the wet heat of dueling tongues.

Yes. This. More.

I broke the kiss long enough to pull my sweater off and toss it to the floor, but I kept my T-shirt on. I couldn't take it off. Not yet. But I would. Later. In the dark. Maybe.

When Dillon lifted me, putting those big strong hands under my ass and hoisting me up until our faces were level with one another, I squeaked in surprise. Fuck yeah. Being manhandled was hot. I wrapped my arms and legs around the larger man, loving the way my hardening cock rubbed against Dillon's bulge.

Then my back was pressed against the wall. The surface was cool through the thin fabric of my T-shirt, a sharp contrast to the heat of Dillon's body pressed against mine. I shivered. Or maybe it was the way Dillon rolled his hips that was making me tremble.

"Fuck." I groaned the word against his lips before ripping my mouth away. "I'm going to come in my pants if you keep doing that."

Dillon huffed out a soft laugh as he mouthed the side of my neck and did that thing with his hips again. My whole body burned and ached and felt so damn good. If I didn't know better, I'd almost think my magic was coming to life, that's how good Dillon was making me feel. I wanted to laugh at how insanely happy that made me. Maybe there was hope. And maybe Dillon was responsible for that hope.

"Bedroom," I demanded. "Now."

"Yes, sir," Dillon said.

He was probably teasing, but those words amped my arousal to another level. I hadn't even known I could be so turned on without having my dick touched.

Dillon's long thick fingers squeezed my ass again as he lifted me away from the wall and carried me to my bed. I offered a quick thank you to my earlier self from three years ago who'd picked out the king-sized bed and another to my earlier self of this morning who'd changed the sheets.

When we arrived at the side of the bed, I expected Dillon to toss me on the bed, but he didn't. He lowered me to the mattress with gentle care and I didn't know what to do with that. I hated being coddled. My mother and brother had smothered me with care after my magic had been assaulted. But Dillon didn't know about that. That wasn't why he was being gentle and careful. It was almost like he thought I was precious.

But I wasn't breakable, and I refused to be treated like I was. I was a survivor, and I could take whatever I was dealt. Even in bed.

I nipped at Dillon's bottom lip and bit down until I tasted blood.

Dillon shuddered against me. And then the big guy was moving, pushing clothes aside. His large warm hands slid under the hem of my shirt.

I froze.

Then Dillon froze too.

I looked down. Shit. My hands were wrapped around his forearm so tightly I'd probably cut off the blood to his hand. But I couldn't let go. I couldn't let him under my shirt. I didn't want him to touch those scars or see them. Either of those things sounded horrible.

My heart pounded.

He sniffed the air and winced at what I imagined was a whole lot of fear in the air. Dillon moved to pull away, but I couldn't let go of him. I didn't want him to leave. I just didn't want him to touch me.

I was so fucked up.

Dillon rolled off me to lie beside me on the bed. He didn't try to extricate his arm from my hold. I pulled his hand out of my shirt but even then I didn't let go of him. It was weird, right, to hold on to someone's arm like this? I half wanted to pull his large hand to my body and curl around it like it was a teddy bear. I didn't. We stayed like that for several long minutes as my heart slowly calmed. Dillon didn't speak, like he understood I needed a minute to get control before I could do anything else.

Eventually I loosened my grip on his arm, but I still didn't release him. I brushed my fingers over his skin. I'd probably given him bruises. And not the fun kind.

I sighed. Although maybe it sounded a bit like a sob.

"It's okay, little witch," Dillon whispered. "Everything is okay."

I couldn't make myself speak. Or nod. Or do anything except trail my fingers up and down his muscular arm. My ex, he'd been a lot smaller than Dillon, and he'd done so much damage. It was peculiar how I wasn't afraid of Dillon, even with all his muscles and his massive body and the legendary supernatural strength that came with him being a hellhound.

I knew he would never hurt me. I didn't understand why I felt that way. Sure, I could pretend it had to do with Van knowing I'd brought Dillon home with me. After all, he probably wouldn't hurt me even if he wanted to, since we'd be seeing the Chief of Police again tomorrow.

But that wasn't why I trusted him not to hurt me.

This stranger—this beautiful sexy man—made me feel safe and secure. It was as if the Eternal Magic had reached inside me and brushed away my fears so I could let this man close.

So why the hell had I freaked out on him?

"Did I hurt you?" Dillon asked softly.

"No." I rushed to get the word out.

"Can you tell me what happened? So I don't do it again?"

Dillon thought there might be another time. I shuddered in relief and pressed my face to his palm. He cradled my head in his hand. I wasn't ready to talk about that tonight, so I shook my head slightly.

"It's not you." I forced the words out.

I'd thought that would make Dillon relax, but instead his body became more rigid. "Did someone else hurt you?"

The rumble of menace rolling through his question made me smile.

"If someone hurt you, I will kill them."

At least that's what I thought he'd said. To be honest, his words were difficult to understand because his voice had dropped into a low growl.

Had he just threatened to kill for me? And if he did, that probably shouldn't turn me on, right? Then I remembered what he'd said earlier… He couldn't lie. I lifted my face away from his hand, needing to see his expression.

The fire of his hellhound blazed brightly in his eyes when my eyes met his. Smoke curled out from his nostrils and mouth. As a fire mage, I'd always loved the scent of smoke and Dillon's embodied everything I loved: a hint of ash, a sweetness of burning applewood, and a classic smokiness that triggered the feelings of warmth and home. The soothing scent reminded me of the bonfires my family used to have in my childhood backyard. They were good memories, ones I'd almost forgotten under the weight of everything that had happened since then.

"Did someone hurt you, Ash?"

I opened my mouth to explain, but I didn't have the energy to talk about all of that tonight. Dillon's warm fingers brushed lightly over my cheeks in a soothing caress.

"I'm sorry," I said.

"We don't have to do anything tonight. Maybe we were going too fast anyway. I'm finding it hard to go slow with you though." His cheeks darkened slightly, and I wondered if that was him blushing.

"Hard?" I couldn't resist poking at the word like a pubescent teen, even though given how I'd stopped everything I should probably have kept my mouth shut.

"Yes." Dillon smiled. "Hard in so many ways."

I smiled back at him, happy that he'd let me try to lighten the mood.

"The things I feel for you." Dillon looked into my eyes. "It feels so right even though we've only just met. I don't want to rush this between us. If you need time, it's okay. Or even if you never want to do *that* with me… I'm here, Ash. For as long as you want me. Unless you've changed your mind."

I swallowed. "I… I feel the same way. Just, uh, maybe

be patient with me. I didn't know I would react like that. I just…"

Dillon took my hand in his and drew it to his lips. He kissed the back of my hand. "It's enough to know you want me too."

"I do," I said, probably a bit too eagerly.

The tension in our bodies seemed to melt as we settled on the bed beside one another. For the next while, we didn't even speak much, just a few words here and there as I traced the length of his thick fingers with mine, or he brushed his fingers through my hair. Then I rested my hand over the center of his chest to feel his heartbeat against my palm while he cupped the back of my neck and squeezed gently. Another delicious cascade of tingles shot through me, and I decided tingles weren't so worrisome after all.

I'd never felt so comfortable with another person.

And before I knew it, my eyes were getting heavy.

"I should go to the couch." He moved to sit up, but I gripped his arm again.

"No. Please, don't go. Hold me while I sleep," I whispered.

He rolled me to my side, then curled up behind me with one of his large arms under my head as a pillow and the other wrapped over me to hold me tightly against his chest. I sighed as his warmth surrounded me.

With a wiggle of my fingers and a whisper of magic, I turned the lights off in my apartment. Feeling the heat of Dillon's body against mine in the darkness made every-thing else that had happened between us seem even more important and intimate. I couldn't remember ever feeling so warm or so safe.

I never would have thought that tonight could have turned out so perfectly.

And as soon as that thought crossed my mind, I worried I'd jinxed things. But how could anything go wrong with Dillon at my side?

Chapter Seven

DILLON

Threatening to kill people probably wasn't the right thing to do, but I'd been absolutely serious when I'd said that to Ash. Thankfully, my little witch hadn't been scared by my promise to him. And it was a promise. Whoever hurt him deserved to suffer.

I didn't need to know the details of what happened to know that much.

At least Ash was with me now and I would make sure nothing ever hurt him again.

His small thin body was curled against me, sheltered in my arms. I was struck by the rightness of holding him, of being with him, of putting my body between him and the rest of the world. I was scared to admit, even to myself, what that meant. Everything with Ash felt too fragile right now. As if acknowledging my suspicions might jeopardize everything.

So I held my thoughts close and Ash even closer.

He slept peacefully in my arms, but I couldn't relax. Not until I knew what had happened to him. Not until I knew what needed to be done to make things right for him. I wanted to squeeze him tight and never let him go, but I forced my arms to remain loose so he wouldn't feel trapped. I sensed he wouldn't like to be confined by anything, especially not a guy he'd just met.

It was strange, then, that he hadn't moved away from me yet.

On the rare occasions when I'd spent a full night with someone, they'd inevitably roll away from me within a few minutes, complaining the heat from my body made them sweaty and uncomfortable. But that wasn't happening with Ash. If anything, he snuggled closer. Having him seek warmth and comfort from me soothed something deep inside me.

How could this feel so right so fast?

I inhaled deeply, pulling the sweet scent of him deep into my lungs. Absorbing this tiny part of him into myself.

I sounded like a lunatic. A stalker. A cannibal.

Just like when my primitive impulses wanted to claim him as mine within the first few minutes of meeting him. And those impulses hadn't subsided. Not one little bit. If anything, they grew stronger the longer I was with him. I couldn't imagine the intensity of what I'd feel for him in a week, a year, a decade…

It was too soon to think like that, but a part of me—that ever-hopeful part that hadn't given up on good in the world and that still remembered what it felt like to have a true home—rejoiced at how perfect things felt with Ash. I hoped I was right about what was causing all of this, even if I couldn't label it yet, not even to myself. The word *mate* —I shivered just at the thought of it—was too precious to even ponder for a millisecond, because if I was wrong…

I closed my eyes, knowing I wouldn't sleep, but savoring the feel of Ash's warm body in my arms. I wanted to memorize everything about this moment. I hoped there would be thousands—no that wasn't enough, I wanted an infinity—of moments like this in our lives, but I wanted to remember everything about this first one.

I'd probably feel the same about the second and the third and—

Danger! My hellhound's warning ricocheted through me.

All happy thoughts scattered. Something was wrong, wrong, wrong…

Was there an intruder? A threat lurking in the night? A shift in the weird magic of this place? I couldn't tell and that only intensified my feeling of *wrongwrongwrong*…

My beast nudged me, urging me to fix what was wrong, but I didn't even know what that was. I inhaled softly, scared of moving too much and waking Ash in case my hellhound was just overreacting. I couldn't scent anything. I strained to hear what might have gotten the attention of my beast. I wanted to partially shift just my ear, but if there was someone here, they would immediately notice my hellhound's flame covered ear in the darkness.

That's when I realized I couldn't hear or smell anything. At all.

I should have scented Ash. I should have heard his steady breaths.

But there was nothing.

It wasn't natural. Someone was using magic to hide themselves. And for me to have picked up on it meant they had to be close. Inside the apartment. Possibly inside this room.

My instincts warred with one another. Half of me wanted to crawl over Ash and protect him from whatever was about to happen. And the other half wanted to attack and deal with the threat—because this was undoubtedly a threat.

My need to destroy any potential danger to my little mage won.

I made a show of rolling away from Ash, as if I was moving in my sleep. I hoped it would be enough to draw the attacker's attention to me. I flung my arm over my eyes, hoping that would be enough to shield my eyes from view when I opened them, because there was no way my eyes weren't lit up like a fucking forest fire right now. My beast surged through my blood, heating my body, ready to shift and destroy any intruder.

Opening my eyes just a sliver was all I needed to do. Two of my former packmates leaned over the bed, one on each side. Their faces were distorted by a half shift. The one closest to me wore a clunky pendant on a thick chain around his neck. The amulet glowed faintly in the dark with a pale icy blue magic.

It wasn't the magic that made me move, though. It was everything else. I didn't need the muted glow of the pendant and the faint light coming in from an outside streetlight to see their gleaming teeth… and the knives in their hands—knives they were lifting over both Ash and me.

Every protective instinct in me fired at once. In an eruption of motion, I rolled over Ash, wrapped my arms around him, then kept tumbling off the other side of the bed. As we fell, we hit one werewolf's legs. The momentum sent him flying backwards.

We landed on the floor. Hard. I did my best to protect Ash from the worst of the impact, making sure my knees and elbows hit the floor first, trying to cradle him against me. Ash went rigid in my arms, and I knew he had to be screaming but I still couldn't hear anything.

I shoved him under the bed to protect him while I dealt with the assholes who'd planned to kill us while we slept.

Shifting to my hellhound form took mere seconds. The flickering light of the fire coating my body made ghoulish patterns undulate across the surfaces in the room. The wolf who'd been on the other side of the bed looked stunned. The knife he'd been holding was embedded in the mattress, right where I'd been sleeping. The wolf closest to me was still clambering to his feet.

I roared into the silence, but no sound broke through the strange magic.

The look on my face must have been enough, though. The wolf furthest from me—the one who wore the pendant —blinked once, then ran for the door. The closest one wasn't so lucky. I opened my mouth and grabbed his leg, sinking my teeth into his flesh. I expected the tangy taste of blood to coat my tongue, but there was nothing. I didn't taste anything. If I hadn't felt the denim of his jeans against my tongue and the bulk of his leg keeping my mouth from closing, I would have thought I'd missed and was chewing on air.

Then, in a strange sensation, like when I'd last driven through the mountains, my ears popped. Suddenly, every-thing—sound, taste, and smell—rushed over me again. The guy with the amulet was about eight feet away now, so that had to be the limit of the talisman's strange magic. The scent of burning flesh filled my lungs as my fire ate away at the werewolf where my fire met his skin and entered his body. His screams filled the darkness. His boiling blood spurted across my tongue.

When he fainted, probably from the pain, I let go and jumped toward the door. There was still a chance I could catch the other bastard.

Before I breached the threshold, though, Ash's whim-pers stopped me.

I spun around and scanned the room for him. He was still under the bed where I'd shoved him. When I ducked down to peer under the bed, my hellhound's fire penetrated the darkness to reveal his huddled form. He was a shaking, trembling, whimpering ball.

In the next moment, I shifted to my human form and flipped the mattress and box spring off the bedframe so I could get to him. As soon as I tossed the mattress aside, he erupted upward like a vengeful specter and shot across the room to the wolf I'd caught.

Sparks blasted from his fingers like firecrackers, and I was sure he'd use his considerable magic to incinerate the wolf. Instead, he kicked and clawed.

"Who the fuck do you think you are?" Ash screamed at the motionless wolf.

I had half a mind to let him take out his frustration and fear on the intruder, but I couldn't let him hurt himself.

"Ash," I whispered as I inched toward him. I didn't want to scare him any more than he already was. "You're safe, little witch. You're safe."

Then Ash lunged at me. At first, I feared he was attacking me too, mistaking me for one of the intruders, but then his arms and legs wrapped around me with surprising strength as he clung to me. His body trembled against mine. I slid to the floor and held him close. The sparks he'd been shedding subsided the longer I held him.

When he finally calmed, he pulled back and waved his hand through the air, releasing a nearly imperceptible flash of magic. The overhead light came on. I grunted and squinted under the bright light. Ash crawled off me and motioned for me to stand with him. As soon as I was on my feet, he eyed me critically. He patted my body, looked me up and down, and then walked around me to do the same with my back.

As he moved around me, he muttered "What the fuck? What the fuck?" over and over again.

"I'm fine, little witch," I said. Although I wished the second wolf would come back to try to finish the job. I had a few things I'd like to say and do to him.

I'd always assumed calmness in the face of a difficult situation to be a hellhound trait. After all, no one would want such a powerful species walking around with a hair trigger, but having someone threaten Ash changed everything. My blood churned through me like molten lava, ready to explode and obliterate anyone in its path.

Still, I couldn't regret staying close to Ash when he needed me.

"Are you sure they didn't hurt you?" Ash circled me again. His fists clenched and unclenched at his sides.

"We should call Van." I reached for his hand and held it gently in mine. He was calmer now, but he wasn't settled yet.

"Answer me."

"I'm sure," I said. "I was lucky I woke when I did. I saw them as they were lifting their knives."

"Fuck." Ash's eyes flashed with a weak crimson light that must be connected to his magic.

Then he swung his attention back to the intruder I had caught. He wrenched himself away from me, and I let him go. He stalked over to the unconscious wolf. He kicked him again. Once. Twice. Three more times.

This time he was shouting something different—something that warmed all those cold, lonely places in my heart. "He is mine. You do not touch him. You do not look at him. I will annihilate you if you try anything against him ever again."

Ash probably would have kept at it, but I pulled him away when I heard the rush of heavy footsteps coming our way.

"Police!" came a shout from the door. "We're coming in. Put your hands up."

Then Van's big body barreled into the room.

Chapter Eight

ASH

To say I was livid was an understatement.

Two ass-wipes had broken into my home and tried to kill us in our sleep. I wanted to go over and kick the shit out of the one Dillon had caught all over again. The guy still hadn't woken up, but no one seemed surprised by that when Dillon explained how he'd been in his hellhound form when he'd bitten him.

Was that normal? I really needed to find out more about hellhounds. Were their bites venomous? Why hadn't the guy's clothes burned off if he'd been exposed to the flames I'd seen dripping from Dillon's fur? And that led to more questions—like why wasn't my apartment burning down?

"So they were from the Red Hills pack?" Van asked.

Dillon nodded. "I'd never been introduced to them —Rob limited my exposure to most of the pack. Said I needed to prove myself first. But I recognized them. Even without being able to scent them."

I gritted my teeth and scowled at the intruder whose leg was being tended to by a first responder. My meager magic had identified the paramedic as a shifter of some kind, maybe a large bird like an emu. He seemed keen to help the wolf, even if he was a murderous bastard.

"They must have followed my scent here." Dillon grimaced. "I should have known they would keep coming after me. I put Ash at risk."

"This isn't your fault," Van said.

"Van's right." I pointed my finger at the unconscious wolf. "It's his fault and it's that asshole Robbie or Rob or whatever his name is… It's his fault too that any of this happened. He sent his minions here. If they'd followed your scent, they'd have known you'd already been to the police station. What did they hope to gain?"

Sparks exploded from the tips of my fingers at the thought of how close those bastards had come to killing Dillon. And me. But mostly I was pissed about the threat to Dillon's life. In the back of my mind, I figured that was because I wasn't ready to deal with the fact that yet another person had tried to kill me in my sleep. Like seriously. What the fuck? Did I have some kind of paranormal bullseye painted on me somewhere?

Van shook his head and glanced at the prisoner. "Maybe he'll tell us."

"I suspect they wanted revenge because I betrayed their alpha," Dillon said.

More sparks shot out of my fingers, but neither Van nor Dillon commented on it. Dillon reached for one of my hands and threaded his fingers through mine. His touch had an unexpectedly calming effect on me. I mean, don't get me wrong, I still wanted to kick the crap out of the wolf in my bedroom, but Dillon's touch reminded me we were both safe.

"If Dillon hadn't woken when he did…" This time, in addition to the sparks, the lights in the room flickered.

"Hey," Dillon soothed as he rubbed the back of my hand. "You're safe now. We both are."

I growled at the implication we might not have been, but my anger wasn't helping. I knew that. So I forced myself to take a deep breath.

"Did you get the other one?" Dillon asked.

"My deputies are out hunting for him now, but I don't expect them to find much."

"I want them charged," I said.

"Of course." Van looked affronted at the implication they wouldn't be charged. "If we don't find the other wolf in town, I'm going to the pack lands. If he's there, I'll find him."

"*If* he is?" I swallowed and looked at Dillon. "Do you think Rob guy would turn him out?" I couldn't call him Robbie anymore, even if that was what everyone else in Willow Lake called him. Robbie sounded like the name of a cute and innocent little kid and that guy was anything but cute or innocent.

He rubbed his chin. "Yeah. Probably. It'll give him the opportunity to deny he knew anything about the attack."

"So this guy's our only hope of tying this to Rob?" I gestured toward the still unconscious wolf in my bedroom.

We all looked at the wolf in question. Hopefully he'd wake soon. I was ready for this to be over.

"Do we need to stay somewhere else tonight?" Dillon asked.

Van shook his head. "I'll leave someone outside, but I don't think they'll be back." Then he looked at me. "You should put some extra security on your door tomorrow."

Extra security. I shivered. I'd only just gotten to the point where I didn't move furniture in front of my door every night. Now these bastards had destroyed all that progress in one night.

More sparks burst from my fingertips.

If I still lived with my coven, they probably would have been here already to help ward the place. But I didn't live with them anymore. They'd been amazing during my recovery, but when I'd moved to Willow Lake, I'd needed my independence and I hadn't kept in touch with them like I probably should have. It'd taken a long time to accept that what had happened with my ex was an isolated incident, but once I had, I'd needed space.

Although perhaps not too much space. After all, I lived in an apartment complex for a reason.

Living in an apartment was what had saved me before and I wasn't a complete idiot. I took precautions. I led a cautious life. Well, until I invited a stranger to my house on an impulse. And now look what happened. If I told my mom about this attack and asked for the coven's help, she wouldn't show up with anyone from the coven. Nope, she'd be outside my apartment in two hours with a U-Haul and a stack of packing boxes.

So I guess that meant I was going to the hardware store

instead. Maybe one of those swing bar door guards like hotel rooms had would work. But let's face it, if a pack of wolves wanted in, there wasn't much I could do to stop them.

"Yeah, okay," I said.

By the time Van and his people left, I was crashing. The adrenaline that'd flooded my system during the attack was long gone. I'd eaten all the sugary things Van had handed me. I'd allowed Dillon to wrap me in two thick blankets and cuddle with me on the couch. But now I was done.

I stood at the threshold of my bedroom and stared at the mess. It wasn't as bad as I'd expected. The mattress and box spring were still flopped over, leaning against the far wall of the room where Dillon had tossed them after the attack. And the cat figurine Paws had given me for my last birthday was on its side on top of my dresser. I was surprised it hadn't broken since the wolf had fallen against it when Dillon bit him.

I swallowed and edged into the room.

I expected to find a large blood stain on the floor. Dillon had bitten him, after all. But there wasn't one. So where had the blood gone? My stomach turned as I realized Dillon must have swallowed it down. No wonder I'd smelled toothpaste on him when he'd returned from the bathroom earlier.

"Let's get this sorted," Dillon said softly from behind me.

I nodded and shuffled to the dresser first. I righted the figurine while Dillon moved the mattress and box spring back into place. The sheets, pillows and blankets were a jumbled tangle on the floor. It only took ten minutes to make the bed. It would have been faster, but I'd spent most of that time fingering the jagged edge of the brand-new knife holes in my bedding and mattress.

"That…" I swallowed. "That was meant for you."

"But they didn't get me or you."

I nodded, but I couldn't stop old familiar fears from skating over me. I ducked down to look under the bed, even though mere minutes ago I'd seen exactly what was under there. Of course, nothing was hiding there except dust bunnies and a wayward sock. Still, I needed to see. To check.

Dillon didn't say anything.

Then I moved to the closet. I opened the sliding doors one way, then the other. I pushed my clothes around, checking both corners. I looked under them. Nothing was there. My brain knew I wouldn't find anything there, but I'd needed to look.

Dillon followed when I returned to the living room.

I checked under and behind every piece of furniture and curtain. I even looked inside the kitchen cupboards.

Of course, nothing was there either.

Then I confirmed the deadbolt was engaged. Maybe if I'd used it instead of just the one on my doorknob it would have delayed the wolves, but I doubted it. Three times I pulled on the doorhandle to make sure it wouldn't give. Then Dillon helped me slide my living room chair in front of the door. Given how it filled up the narrow hallway, I doubted anyone would be able to get in very easily with that in place. Then, when we returned to the bedroom, we moved the dresser in front of that door.

When that was done, a smidgeon of my anxiety eased.

Dillon took the side of the bed closest to the door again. We silently crawled under the covers. When his arms wrapped around me, I trembled. He squeezed me tight, and I closed my eyes. He had saved me tonight. Saved us both, really.

I was safe with him.

But I needed to keep him safe too and I'd failed. Dillon had come to my home and been attacked. I hadn't been able to protect him. If my magic wasn't damaged, maybe things would have been different. But as it was, I was useless.

That hole in the mattress had almost been a hole in his chest.

And I couldn't quit thinking about that.

Chapter Nine

DILLON

Morning came too soon.

I doubted either Ash or I slept more than a few minutes at a time after Van left. Maybe it was even less than that. I consciously listened to everything, making sure nothing was out of place. Then I'd sniff, checking that all the right scents were in the air.

And then I'd get irritated.

There were too many scents in Ash's bedroom—all those strangers trampling through his inner sanctum as they dealt with that stupid wolf—but at least I understood why they were there. Still, that didn't mean I wouldn't be setting aside some time later today to rub my scent all over his stuff. I might get him to do the same, so our scents were mingled together in his bedroom.

Hopefully that would help calm my beast, because right now the only thing keeping me from shifting and hunting down the wolf who got away was knowing how much Ash needed me.

He'd clung to me the whole night.

Well, it was probably more accurate to say we'd clung to one another.

It wasn't sexual. We hadn't even kissed after we crawled into bed and held each other tight.

Rest hadn't come easily. We'd each flipped and flopped through the night, always moving slowly as we tried not to disturb the other. And then, when we settled, we cuddled up again. That happened over and over and over.

As dawn approached, my hellhound's anxiety eased. I doubted the wolves would attack in daylight. Their magical amulet might let them move without being scented or heard, but it hadn't stopped me from seeing them. That lessening sense of worry was the only reason we were cuddling as we were now, with Ash's body blanketing mine and his head resting on my chest. I liked having him draped over me like I was his favorite pillow, but I would never have been okay with it during the night. When the shadows had cloaked the room, I'd needed to know I was between him and any possible threat.

What a long fucking night.

I stifled a yawn as I brushed a kiss against his hair. I resisted the urge to squeeze him tight in case he'd finally managed to fall into a restful sleep.

As I breathed in his scent, a little more of my anxiety uncoiled. His body fit so perfectly with mine. Actually, everything about him fit with me. That had to mean something, right? Like he was destined to be mine.

And I'd nearly lost him.

As much as I hadn't been willing to admit it last night, I could now. Ash was special. He could be my one and only, because that was the only explanation for my overwhelming and immediate reaction to him. I was becoming more convinced of that by the moment. And I'd be damned if some fuckhole was going to take him from me.

"You okay?" Ash whispered.

I grunted and squeezed him.

"You went all tense," he said.

"I'm fine. Just getting angry about what happened."

He nodded against my chest. "We should check in and get an update from Van."

Yeah. We probably should. I didn't like the odds of hearing what I wanted to hear, but I needed to know. And we also needed to buy more locks for Ash's door. This was a supernatural town so hopefully the local store carried more than generic human security hardware.

But, as Ash wiggled against me in the quiet of the morning, my mind strayed from thoughts of security and would-be wolf assassins. The clothes caught between our bodies were hot and sweaty, but I didn't mind that. I was a hellhound. I loved heat. But I would have loved it even more if nothing separated us at all. I wanted his heated and sweaty skin rubbing against mine. I wanted to lick the perspiration from his body. I wanted to make him even hotter.

I trailed my hand down his back, loving the way he arched into my touch. He hummed quietly and turned his face toward my neck. The warmth of his breath whispered across my skin as his lips brushed against me.

Every part of me was awake now. Including my dick.

"I thought you wanted to get ready." I angled my head to give him better access to my neck. Fuck, his lips felt good on me.

"Later," he murmured.

Chapter Ten

ASH

I had been thinking about being naked with Dillon all night long. Every single minute I was awake, anyway. Even the minutes that were interrupted by vengeful thoughts about the wolves ended with me imagining how I could reward this sexy man who'd saved me or how I wanted to go out, hunt down the wolf who got away, and drag him back here to present him to Dillon as a gift.

And what kind of fucked up thought was that? I wasn't a shifter. I was a mage. Mages weren't supposed to want to kill and maim for our mates.

Mates. That word also kept repeating in my head.

"I want you," I whispered against his throat. His pulse quickened under my mouth at my words, and I smiled.

"Are you sure? We don't have to…"

Last night's seduction hadn't gone to plan. I'd panicked. But, at some point during everything that had happened after that, something had changed for me. Letting him see my scars didn't seem as scary anymore.

And that felt big.

Important.

Monumental.

And absolutely, perfectly right.

If I still met with my therapist, this would definitely be a talking point.

No one had seen my scars in years, and I preferred it that way. The few times I'd had sex in the last few years had been the kind of sex where everyone stayed mostly dressed, dropped their pants to expose the necessary parts, and didn't ask for names. I hadn't loved doing it, but I hadn't been ready to make myself any more vulnerable than that either. As much as I'd always craved having more with someone in all the years leading up to the attack, I'd found dozens of ways to talk myself out of pursuing anything more serious since then. Finally, I'd just given up. Celibacy wasn't so bad. Really.

And now Dillon had somehow gotten past all my defenses, almost from the moment I'd seen him on the night-cloaked road. Maybe fate really had brought us together.

I swallowed hard and sat up so I could see his face. He was gorgeous. A sense of rightness filled me at seeing him lying rumpled in my bed. I wanted to crawl all over his big body like flames on kindling. He didn't move, he just lay still watching me, like he understood I needed a bit of space to take this step.

My fingers fumbled at the hem of my shirt.

"So…" I looked away from him to stare at the weave of the sheets. "I… um… I…"

"Hey," he said softly. "Whatever it is, I'm going to be okay with it. Okay? Trust me. Nothing you can show me will put me off."

I nodded. He could say that now, but he hadn't seen them yet. My scars were ugly. Hideous. And if seeing them made him pity me like everyone else who'd seen them, I wasn't sure what I'd do.

"I have…" My voice broke. I cleared my throat. "I have some scars."

"Okay," he said slowly.

I needed to know what he was thinking, and his one-word response didn't help. I forced myself to look up and meet his eyes, which were blazing with his hellhound's fires. They seemed to do that when he was emotional.

"I thought I should warn you. They're kind of…" I swallowed hard. "Well, not nice to look at."

"Your scars won't change how much I want you." He spoke with such sincerity, I ached to believe him.

I curled my fingers around the bottom of my shirt. Before I could lift it, he reached out to stop me.

"You don't have to do this, Ash," he said. "Let's do whatever makes you the most comfortable. If you want to keep your shirt, then keep your shirt. If you want to do this in the dark, we can put a blanket over the window and keep the lights off. But just listen to me for a second. I know you don't believe me even though you know I can't lie, but I promise you, nothing you can show me will make me desire you any less than I do right now."

My eyes burned but I sucked in a breath and grabbed

my shirt with more determination this time. I managed to lift it, just an inch or so. Then I froze. I didn't move. Dillon didn't move.

The longer I sat there with just a few inches of my stomach exposed, the more I felt the possibility of sex slip away.

Dillon put his hands on mine and pulled them away from my shirt.

"We don't have to do this," he said.

"But I want to…"

"Have you done this before?"

"Like sex?" I asked as my cheeks heated. I didn't know why. It wasn't like I was a virgin, but I hadn't really ever just talked about sex. My former lovers and I had just got on with getting it on. "Yes."

"So what's different with me?" He tried to keep his face blank, but I could tell it was an effort. And I could also tell under that carefully neutral look that I'd hurt him. I couldn't let him think I didn't want him, because the truth was I wanted him too much.

"I don't usually get undressed. They're usually quick and dirty hookups."

Dillon cleared his throat and the flames blazed brighter in his eyes. Okay. He obviously didn't like that too much. Was it because I'd talked about having sex with other people? Because, honestly, I could understand that. I didn't want to think about him getting it on with anyone else either.

"I shouldn't have asked." Dillon clenched and unclenched his jaw.

"I don't want that with you."

His eyes widened.

"I mean... I don't want quick and dirty. I want..." I didn't know how to talk about what I wanted. I wasn't even sure I'd figured it out myself. It was way too early in our relationship—actually, could we even put a label on whatever was happening between us? It was too soon.

"So don't undress."

I blinked at him. "I mean we could do that, but... I thought... It just seemed..."

"Whatever is going on between us feels special to me too," he said, as if reading my mind. "But we don't have to have sex for it to be like that. Or, if we do, we don't have to be naked, not if it makes you feel uncomfortable."

I sat back and stared at him. "Are you sure?"

"We have time. We just met... Although I'd swear it feels like I've known you my whole life, we can't expect to share all our secrets within hours of meeting." He squeezed my hands, which I'd forgotten he'd been holding. "But when you are ready, I'll be here for you, and I'll listen to whatever you want to share."

I blinked away the stinging in my eyes. He was right. It did feel like we'd known one another longer, but I'd only picked him up from the side of the road last night. I didn't understand how it could feel like so much more than that. And it was pretty wild that he was feeling the same way. Did that mean he was sticking around for a while so we could get to know one another?

Was it too soon to want that and more?

My past had taught me to take things slowly and to be cautious, but Dillon was making me break all my rules. I didn't want to slow down, even though I swear I could hear my former therapist in my head saying if I wasn't ready to share this part of myself with Dillon, maybe I wasn't ready to have sex with him. But she'd have been wrong. So fucking wrong.

"So you'd be okay if I kept my shirt on?"

"Whatever you need."

I flung myself into his arms and we fell back onto the mattress. I kissed him. We both moaned.

And then he was pulling at the rest of my clothes, and I was pulling at his. The ones that didn't immediately obey were ripped away until we were naked. I refused to think about my scars anymore or the fact that he was carefully avoiding my shirt. Besides, I had better things to think about… like trying to touch every part of him.

Spells and curses, this guy… He was perfection, like every one of my wet dreams since I hit puberty all rolled up into this god-like man, from his wide shoulders, rippling abs, and muscular thighs to his long thick erection bobbing between us. A pearly bead of precum coated the crown of his cock, and I couldn't resist the temptation to taste him. I reached out and drew my thumb over his flushed skin and wiped away the drop. Dillon shivered and moaned under my touch. Then I locked gazes with him as I raised my thumb to my mouth and licked it clean with my tongue. He tasted like heat and smoke and absolute perfection.

"I want to lick every part of you. Taste you. Memorize you. But later. Right now, I want to fuck," I said.

"Top or bottom?"

"You'd bottom?" Fuck, I'd done it, hadn't I? I'd gone and made an assumption about Dillon's preferences because of his size. I hated when guys did that to me. "Right. Never mind. Scratch that I asked you that."

"You can ask me anything, little witch." Then Dillon leaned forward until his mouth was at my ear before whispering, "And for the record, I like both. I want both. With you. Want to feel you tight and hot around my dick. Want to feel you deep and thick inside me when you come. Want you all ways. Want to see you lose control over and over because of me. But only if you want that too."

I damn near shot my load. I gripped the base of my cock and squeezed to slow things down. Every insecurity I'd had was gone now. At least for the moment. I wanted him and he wanted me and that was all that was important.

"You in me first. Then we'll see what happens next."

"Yes, sir."

"Fuck, those words…" They did something to me. My body arched against Dillon's.

Dillon laughed like he knew exactly what effect he was having on me. The big guy might say "yes, sir" like I was the boss right now, but it was Dillon who had taken full control of my body and thoughts and desires. But just the suggestion that I was in control eased any lingering anxiety. And apparently I'd needed that.

I threw myself into giving Dillon as much pleasure as I possibly could. We explored and teased and tasted one another until his stomach and the bottom of my shirt were coated in precum.

"Lube?"

"Top drawer." Then I remembered I didn't have condoms. The last time I'd had sex was eons ago and I'd tossed the condoms a few months ago because they'd expired.

But then my brain caught up to what was going on and I relaxed. Sexually transmitted infections weren't a thing for supes—magic was apparently a bit of a cure-all in that regard. Until Dillon, I hadn't been able to stomach the idea of being with a supe—despite how I'd drooled over a few of the guys around town—so my few hookups over the years had been with humans. With them, condoms were expected. Even my ex, when he'd been pretending to be human, had demanded we use condoms. Most supes only used condoms to prevent pregnancy. As a gay guy, I didn't need to worry about that. But we still needed to talk about it.

"Uh… I don't have condoms… I mean I know we don't need any, because you know… magic and all that… but I thought I should tell you." I'd never knowingly been with a supe before, so my pulse raced at the idea of Dillon being bare inside me.

Dillon's breath caught. Fire danced in his eyes. I could feel his body heat rise even more. "If you are okay with it…"

"I am." I nodded quickly. "And I definitely have lube. So much lube. Hey, don't judge. The ginormous bottle was on sale."

I eyed Dillon's erection again. And my penny-pinching ways were now paying off because, yes, we'd need lube. Lots of it. None of my previous lovers were so generously endowed. Hell, even my dildos weren't that long and thick.

"Hey," Dillon said, drawing my attention again. "We don't have to. Not now. Not ever. Not if you don't want to."

"Hell, no," I said shaking my head. "We're not stopping now, big guy." I palmed Dillon's cock. "Just prep me good."

Dillon nodded, then a sly grin played at his mouth, and I knew exactly what he was going to say before he whispered those two little words, "Yes, sir."

"Shit. The things you do to me." My cock bobbed. I'd never wanted to be in control in the bedroom before, but maybe that had changed since my ex too. Or maybe it was just Dillon and the way he looked at me when he said those two words. Like he'd give me the world, all I had to do was ask.

Then Dillon's lubed fingers slid down to my ass and all thought ended again. I couldn't look away from his eyes as he rubbed and massaged my opening, getting it slick and wet. When the tip of the first finger pushed inside, I groaned, closed my eyes, and grabbed my knees to open myself to his touch.

"Yes, keep going," I urged.

I lost track of time as Dillon prepped me, rocking his fingers in and out and sweeping against that sweet spot deep inside my body until I was trembling and begging "now, now, now." Dillon wouldn't be rushed though.

When he finally pulled his fingers away, my eyes snapped open to see the hellhound staring at my opening with flames dancing in his eyes. A faint scent of smoke filled the air around us. Dillon was a predator, probably one of the strongest shifters alive, and it was sexy as fuck to have someone that powerful in my bed, staring at me like he wanted to devour me.

"Now, Dillon." I started to flip over, but he grabbed my leg and stopped me.

"I want you on your back, so I can see your face."

Dillon grabbed a pillow. I lifted my hips as the hellhound shoved it under me. Then I grabbed my knees and pulled them to my chest again, exposing myself to him. Dillon moaned. One of his fingers waltzed over my dick and balls, until they ended at my hole again, as if he couldn't stop himself from touching me.

"Fuck me," I demanded.

"So bossy." Dillon smirked but walked forward on his knees until his thighs touched me.

My body tensed in anticipation, and I willed myself to relax.

"If you tell me to stop, I'll stop," Dillon said. "Doesn't matter what's happening. I'll stop, okay."

I didn't know what to do with all the care and time Dillon was taking with me. We may have only known one another for a handful of hours, but this was more than just a meaningless fuck. Our chemistry was astronomical, but these feelings he was coaxing out of me were making me squirm… What was I supposed to do with them? Feelings led to mistakes—mistakes that could shatter me all over again. I squelched those thoughts before they could fester into something more. I had a sexy hellhound in my bed; I had better things to think about.

"Enough with the talk," I said. "Fuck me already."

"Yes, little witch." Dillon didn't smirk this time, he just reached forward and swept the sweaty hair from my forehead. Then he leaned down and brushed the softest and sweetest kiss over my mouth. "I'm going to make you feel so good. Trust me."

And even though I had every reason to never trust anyone again, I suspected the hellhound was going to break down my every defense and protection. And, at this moment, I wasn't even sure I cared.

He sat back again. Without another word, he angled his cock toward my body with one hand and grabbed one of my hands with the other. Then, with our gazes locked on one another, he pushed inside with one slow, deep, smooth thrust. After so much prep, there was only the slightest whisper of discomfort as my body stretched to welcome Dillon inside, but the rest? That was pure pleasure.

My body sang. My magic even seemed to erupt from the place it used to live inside my chest as whirlwinds of fiery colors spun around us. I swore Dillon's magic ignited too, rising in a blast of dancing flame-like hues to join with mine. I'd never seen a shifter's magic like this before, but I didn't question what I saw. Wispy ribbons of orange, yellow and red undulated together until I didn't know which parts were from me and which were from him. It was breathtaking.

My magic had never done anything like that before, even when I was whole.

Dillon's body rocked into mine deeper with each stroke. Some part of me wanted him deeper still, until we were joined so completely there was no telling where he ended and I began. His hellhound was close to the surface too—flames filled his eyes, puffs of smoke heaved from his nostrils, and the tips of his fingers changed into blunt claws where they dug into my hips.

My name fell from Dillon's lips over and over again, punctuated only with deep, guttural groans.

Unspoken promises and hopes and joy filled me until I felt ready to burst with them. How could one man have such an impact on me? How was this so right?

Then I was coming, and Dillon was leaning over me and shuddering through his release too. Instinct too powerful to fight had me turning my head, baring my neck. Then, as if answering my unspoken primal invitation, Dillon's razor-sharp teeth pierced my skin where my neck met my body.

The world around us exploded in an array of magic and heat and bliss before peaceful blackness enveloped me.

Chapter Eleven

DILLON

My hellhound apparently didn't care about consent. The fucking Neanderthal.

I licked the side of Ash's neck where I'd bitten him and waited for him to wake up. The spot where my teeth had punctured his skin was already closed and fading. Thank fuck. My cheeks heated as I relived the moment I'd lost control of my beast. When Ash had tilted his head and exposed his neck, the instinct to bite overrode every other thought. I'd never bitten anyone during sex before—never even felt the tiniest bit tempted to do that—but something about this mage was awakening primitive urges to mark him as mine and keep him safe.

My hellhound nuzzled Ash's neck again, happier than he'd ever been. If I was in my shifted form, he'd be bouncing around like a puppy, wagging his damn tail.

Fuck. How would I stop the beast from doing it again?

Would Ash even want to have another round of sex

with someone who'd used him as a chew toy? And that was my real worry—what if I'd destroyed my chances with him? I should have asked first, but in that moment, seeing Ash bare his neck to me and feeling our magic envelop us, I'd lost control. My instincts overtook everything else, and I closed the loop of power between us.

Would Ash forgive me?

I shivered. If I ruined my chance with this cute little witch because my hellhound became a greedy and primitive bastard during sex, I'd never forgive myself. This was the closest I've ever come to feeling a real connection to someone. Destroying this fragile, tentative sliver of a chance to realize my dreams and find a home with someone amazing would devastate me.

It was probably too fast to feel so connected to him— no, there was no *probably* about it. It *was* too fast to be thinking the things I was thinking. But in all my years on this earth, I'd never found another person who made me feel this way. Being attacked last night had just amplified and accelerated my feelings for him, but they'd started as soon as I'd seen him on that road out in the woods.

I pressed my face into his neck, savoring the way our scents mingled on his skin. I also loved the way his body was sandwiched between me and the mattress. My hellhound hummed contentedly, knowing any threat would have to go through me to get to Ash. But I was too heavy to stay on top of him, no matter how much it felt right to shelter him against me.

I rolled us to our sides.

Ash's T-shirt had ridden up his stomach to reveal the edge of a nasty looking scar. I carefully tugged it back down. I wanted to tug it off, because it was covered in his release, but he wasn't ready to share that with me yet and I could wait. That little glimpse of his scars didn't dampen my need for this man one little bit—not that I'd thought it would.

But the need to destroy whoever had hurt him burned inside me.

I wanted to know more. I wanted to ask him questions about what had happened, but I needed to wait for him to tell me. If I pushed him on this, I could easily drive him away.

I couldn't screw this up.

How did people build relationships? How was I going to woo this little witch and show him what an amazing connection we could have together? Even in my limited experience, I knew biting the guy the first time we had sex probably wasn't the right way.

I used the corner of the sheet to clean the skin I could see on Ash's body, then I did the same to mine. I should probably have gone to the bathroom and gotten a warm, wet cloth, but I didn't want to let Ash go, even for that short of a time. I needed to be with him the moment he woke.

Ash's breathing changed as he twitched and rolled toward me. Him seeking me out was a good sign, right? Or was he so out of it he didn't know what he was doing yet? I held my breath and hugged Ash loosely, unable to stop touching him, but not wanting to scare him by making him feel trapped or confined.

His long, dark eyelashes fluttered as he opened his pale gray-green eyes. He smiled at me, then snuggled closer and pushed his face into my chest.

"Hey," Ash whispered.

"Um, Ash?"

He pulled back to look at my face. "What's wrong?"

My heart hammered in my chest. "I'm so sorry. I'm sorry I bit you without talking to you first."

"Huh?" Ash reached up and touched the place where I had sunk my teeth. The marks were still there, slightly pink. By tonight, they should have faded completely, but that didn't matter. They shouldn't have been there in the first place. "Why? What does it mean? I thought that story about shifters biting people to claim them as a mate was a bogus myth. Are you saying it isn't? Did you mate me and ruin me for anyone else? Are we shifter married now?"

"What? No." I shook my head. "I may not know a lot about mating practices, but I know that much. We aren't linked any more now than we were before, except for, you know, having just shared something amazing."

"So why the apology?"

"I bit you," I said slowly. I was no better than whoever had hurt him before. I'd taken from him without consent. He just looked at me with a puzzled frown, so I continued. "Without asking. Like a rabid dog or something."

"Yeah, but it was hot, right? I mean, I've never passed out during sex before. It was intense and…" He grinned goofily. "You may have ruined me."

I blinked. "So you aren't… uh… angry with me for doing that?"

"Hell no. I'm trying to figure out if I have enough energy to do it again."

A bark of startled laughter erupted from me. I grabbed

Ash tight and pressed my face into his neck to hide my unexpected tears from him. I'd thought I'd ruined every-thing, but maybe I hadn't. This little mage was perfection —or maybe it was just that he was perfect for me. He shouted in surprise at being manhandled into a hug, but then he relaxed against me and sighed. As my panic ebbed away, I became aware of the way his legs tangled with mine and the way he wiggled closer. We should be getting out of bed and dealing with all the shit that had been stirred up the night before, but lingering here with Ash sounded a hell of a lot more fun.

"And? What's the verdict?"

"Not yet..." Ash yawned as his thin fingers drew circles over my skin. "But I want to."

After several long minutes of cuddling in silence, the air between us seemed to change.

"What are you thinking about?" I finally asked.

Another long stretch of silence.

"Did you feel my magic?" Ash's question was barely audible.

I didn't know why, but I instantly understood this was an important question for Ash. Normally, I'd answer with a simple yes but I sensed Ash was asking for a specific reason.

"The air was singing with it. It was beautiful. It's what triggered the bite, I think."

"What do you mean?"

"I've heard rumors, well, they were more like fairy tales, but after tonight I wonder if there was more truth in them than I'd thought." I rubbed Ash's back, loving the feel of his body under my palm—even if he was still covered by a T-shirt. "Sometimes, when two supes come together—"

"Wait. Are you giving me some supernatural birds and bees talk?" Ash snorted. "I suffered through the requisite sex talk with my mother when I hit puberty. I don't need another."

"You asked."

"Fine, fine," Ash said, still sounding amused. "Go on. When two supes love each other very much…" His words trailed off and his body tensed. "I mean… well, not that you love me. Ha, ha. No, I was just kidding. Yeah, okay. Let's forget I said anything. Please continue. You were saying?"

I smiled. I figured I'd be doing that a lot around this little witch—*my* little witch. Because although Ash was right and we weren't at the I-love-you stage yet, it didn't seem like such an outlandish idea that we could get there.

Or maybe I was being optimistic because Ash hadn't freaked out about the bite.

"When people are compatible, I've heard there can be a power exchange during sex. When I bit you, it completed a loop between us. My ejaculation in you, your blood in me."

"Ejaculation? Did you just say the word ejaculation?" Ash snickered. "Is this high school biology class?"

"I'm being serious." I pinched Ash's side softly, making the mage squirm and laugh.

"Alright, alright," Ash said. "What else?"

I shrugged. "I don't know. I've never done it before. But I think the part where our magic surrounded us and blended together was the next level of the same thing."

Ash jolted upright, out of my arms. "Wait. What did you say a minute ago? Something about an exchange? What did you mean?" He rubbed his chest through his T-shirt. "Oh, no."

The air stirred between us, and I knew it was Ash's magic.

"Ash? What's going on?"

"Are you okay? Can you still shift?"

"What do you mean? Of course I can."

"No." Ash scrambled out of bed. "Don't brush this off." He put his hands on his slim hips, just below the hem of his T-shirt, not bothering to cover his bare lower half. I sensed his blatant display of nudity wasn't typical, but in his agitated state he didn't seem to notice he wasn't fully dressed. "Get out of bed and show me that you're okay. Show me your hellhound."

"I'm okay. I feel fine," I said as I rolled out of bed and climbed to my feet. "I will shift for you, so you can see that, but then we need to have a conversation about what's going on. Just stand back okay. My hellhound is covered in fire. Your possessions will be okay, but my fire will burn any living being and I don't want you to get hurt. Okay?"

Ash nodded sharply as he retreated until his back hit the wall. Then his fingers dug into his hips with what seemed like bruising force as his foot bounced with impatience.

I kept my eyes on him as I let my hellhound form roll over my body. My hands became paws. My jaw elongated. My skin itched as black fur, tipped in fire, covered my body.

Ash stared at me. "Are you okay? Was all that normal?

Did anything feel off? Was your shift slower or harder or anything?"

I could have answered in my shifted form—I'd never met a shifter who couldn't talk in their shifted form—but I couldn't soothe my little witch like that. I changed back. "Everything is fine. I'm fine. Everything is the same as always."

Ash hugged his arms over his stomach and sank to his knees. He sucked in a deep breath. "Thank all the deities that ever existed…"

I raced over and scooped the smaller man into my arms. He was trembling. "You're scaring me, little witch."

"Yeah, well, you scared me too. Fuck." He rubbed at his eyes.

"Why are you scared?"

Ash closed his eyes and pressed his face into my chest. "I…" He swallowed hard. "I know I need to tell you. Just… just give me a minute. This… It's hard, okay?"

"Take all the time you need, little witch."

I didn't know what else to do, so I shut my mouth, held on tight to my little mage, and waited.

Chapter Twelve

ASH

I wished I hadn't freaked out, because then this conversation wouldn't be happening, and we would be having another round of amazing sex instead. But if anything had happened to Dillon because of me, how would I live with myself? The short answer was I wouldn't be able to.

Dillon swore he hadn't been harmed, but how could we be one hundred fucking percent certain? Sure, I'd seen him shift, but what if there were lingering effects? I drew in a deep breath and pushed it out slowly. He needed to know.

Okay.

I could do this.

"I come from a long line of mages, so it isn't surprising I inherited an affinity for magic. I am listed as a fire mage in the records housed with my family's coven. As the name suggests, my ability lets me manipulate fire, but also light and, to some extent, electricity." I paused and ducked my head. I couldn't look at Dillon. "It used to be stronger."

Dillon waited for me to continue.

"About seven years ago, I met a guy." I hated that my voice sounded so tremulous, like one of the delicate, fragile ladies in those classic novels my mother made me read because she didn't like the books my teachers chose for class. You know the ones. Women were always dropping dead because their hands were cold, they had a slight case of the sniffles, or something else equally ridiculous. "I was eighteen, brand new to university life, and living away from home for the first time. He swept me off my feet and then things went… sideways."

Dillon didn't say anything. He just kept rubbing soft circles over my back with his large warm hand.

"The investigators called it emotional abuse." It helped to think of it in those terms with no personal pronouns, no overt ownership of what happened. Terms that seemed neutral. Terms that weren't directly linked to me, like it hadn't been me who'd experienced all of that. Even if it had been. "Isolate someone from their family. Gaslight them. Hurt them. Control every part of their lives." I pushed my hand between us to dig my fingers into my sternum, right over the center of my scar tissue. Rubbing it never helped to ease the ache there, but I couldn't stop doing it.

"Who did this to you?" Dillon's growl was filled with smoke.

I shook my head. That wasn't the important part. My ex couldn't hurt Dillon, but I might.

"The relationship lasted ten months, but…" My voice broke. I cleared my throat.

Heat poured off the hellhound's body and it soothed me, made me feel safe—even though every growl, curl of smoke, and flicker of fire revealed the predator living inside Dillon.

"I don't think it would have been so bad, maybe, if he was a regular human like I'd thought. It would have hurt and been difficult, but I think I would have been able to get out of the situation once I saw what was happening, maybe." That's what I liked to tell myself anyway. It was probably a lie to make me feel better, but sometimes lies keep you sane. "But, you see, I hadn't realized he was a witch too. He'd kept that part of himself hidden until the end. People always talk about hindsight being twenty-twenty, or whatever, but it is true. The signs were there. I should have figured it out sooner. I mean, he knew about supes. I should have asked more questions about how he knew the things he did." I swallowed as nausea rolled through me. It happened every time I talked about what happened, even after all this time and countless therapy sessions. "Anyway, I knew something was wrong with my magic. It was weaker than normal. He kept telling me I was being silly and overreacting. That I was tired. Or over-worked. Or not eating enough energy rich foods. Said I was ridiculous to think about bothering a doctor with something so trivial."

I shivered and pressed hard into Dillon's soothing heat. "But I couldn't shake the sense that something was wrong, and I booked an appointment with a local supernatural doctor anyway." It was humiliating to talk about this. Even after all these years. Even after all the counselling. I knew it hadn't been my fault that I'd been targeted. That I was a survivor. But it was still a time in my life I wished I could forget.

"What did the doctor say?"

"I never made it to the doctor, not for that appointment anyway," I said with a sigh. "The day before the appointment, he found out about it. I'd known he was irritated, but I didn't think too much about it. When he said he was staying the night, I didn't suspect a thing. He stayed with me quite often, so it probably would have been stranger if he'd left." I sucked in a breath and let it out slowly. "He attacked in the middle of the night while I was sleeping. By the time I realized what was happening, I didn't have the strength to fight back."

Dillon growled deeply and the scent of smoke grew stronger. I needed to finish this, though, so I steeled myself and pushed on.

"I found out later he'd been stealing my magic from the very beginning, siphoning it off me like a thief in the middle of the night. But that last night? It was bad. He drained me. The courts concluded he meant to kill me."

"A supe can't survive without magic." Dillon's deep voice trembled with his anger, but I knew it wasn't directed at me.

"One of the other tenants in my apartment building was a supe and sensed something was wrong. Said they could feel the energy surge. They called the supernatural rep at the local police department. They caught Chris hauling his shit out of the apartment. I was unconscious but alive."

"You were lucky," Dillon said softly. "What happened to him?"

I sighed and slumped against him. His punishment was almost as difficult to talk about as the attack. "The attack happened right when the Supernatural Council decided to make changes to how they punished people. It used to be that supes were just slapped on the wrist for doing anything except for taking another life. Punishments for anything else fell to a supe's coven or pack or whatever, but with more and more people living outside of traditional supe communities that meant a lot of people were getting away with those non-lethal crimes."

"I remember," Dillon murmured.

"The SC had started experimenting with alternate forms of punishment and incarceration. My ex was one of the first mages to be tried under the new system. They directed a local coven—not the one I grew up in, but another—to strip the magic he stole and bind whatever remained. He… He's been contained at a supernatural penitentiary ever since, but my family continues to fight for a… um… a more permanent solution."

"I agree with your family. A person like that should not be allowed to live. The moment he tried to kill you his life should have been forfeit."

I sighed. That's what my mother and brother said too. I rubbed the scars on my chest. "Honestly, I don't know what to think. Without his magic, he's in a lot of pain. It probably would be more humane to end his life. But I don't want to be the reason he is killed. I don't want his death hanging over me."

"You wouldn't be the reason he was killed," Dillon argued. "He brought this on himself."

"Anyway, it was a long time ago, but my magic has never returned, not fully anyway. I can do small things, but nothing more. And, because my magic is connected to fire, he stole my heat from me too. Ever since that night, I've been cold, always so very cold. It's been years since the attack, and nothing has returned to how it was *before*." I shuddered. I didn't want to say this, but I had to. "Until tonight. Tonight, I felt something. I think I somehow stole magic from you." I curled into him, covering my face in my hands. My body was shaking. "Oh, fuck. I'm just like him."

"Hey, now," Dillon said gently as he tightened his arms around me.

"How can you stand to touch me?" I tried to move away from him, but Dillon didn't let go.

"It's okay, little witch," Dillon soothed. "I think I'm going to have more questions about what you've told me, but they can wait. First, I need to tell you a little bit about hellhounds, okay?"

"Uh… okay?"

"I don't know if you picked up on this in the conversation we had with Van earlier, but hellhounds can't lie," Dillon started. "It isn't a choice. It isn't a moral compass. It's a fact. I've never lived in a pack, but my parents were both hellhounds and although they disappeared when I was young, I still remember some of the things they told me about my heritage or legacy or whatever you want to call it."

"Dillon, I'm so sorry…"

"Thank you, little witch. But I'm telling you this because I think what they told me will be important, for you and for us, if there is or could be an us." Dillon's fingers tightened slightly on me as he spoke, then he paused and seemed to consciously loosen his grip again. "They said the ability to sense lies was like an evolutionary remnant from when hellhounds worked for angels and demons to investigate crimes and dole out punishments." He shrugged. "I mean, I've never met an angel or a demon to ask them, but hellhounds have certain gifts that would help with that role, so it makes sense."

"That's kind of cool, but what does that have to do with what I told you?" That wasn't exactly what I'd wanted to say, but *no wonder I already trust you and, for the first time in my life, I kind of wish I had ovaries so I could have your babies* seemed like a little too much, particularly when he should be wanting to stay far away from me after this.

"I'm getting to that." I could hear the smile in his words. "So we have heightened senses, right? Like any other shifter. But it's a little more involved than that. We can tell if someone is lying or not. And, in our shifted forms, we can see a person's energy, like an aura, but it is focused on their magic. The way my parents explained it to me is like this: When my kind was part of a team of investigators and executioners for supernatural beings, the Eternal Magic gave us the ability to understand the threats around us and take them out if we needed. Hellhounds know how strong other supes are as soon as we shift and see them. It's innate. It helped us protect ourselves as we doled out punishments."

Ah. I understood now. And I was almost scared to ask, but I had to know.

"What do you see when you look at me?" I whispered.

"I see an abundance of magic. It flows around you like a waterfall. Although knowing your affinity is for fire makes sense, because it is like a fiery crimson light."

"But…" That didn't make sense. I hadn't been able to use my magic for almost a decade.

"It's there, little witch," Dillon murmured. "Remember, hellhounds can't lie."

A new feeling shivered through me. Hope. That was what hope felt like.

"I don't know why you don't feel it or can't use it, but it is there. I saw it out on the road when you found me, and I saw it again just now when you asked me to shift."

"So I'm not broken? Or, rather, I'm not broken in the way I thought I was?" That shivering sliver of hope grew a little stronger.

"You aren't broken at all," Dillon said. "You need to find your way home again. That's all. A way to trust yourself. A safe place to access your magic. The loop that formed when I bit you wouldn't have sung like it did if you didn't have such strong magic."

My sight blurred. Shit, I was tearing up. I hadn't cried since I'd first woken up all those years ago and felt a gaping hole where my magic had lived. "It's really there?"

"It's really there," Dillon said. "And I'll say that as many times as you need to hear it to believe it."

"Thank you. I… I probably shouldn't say this so soon —I mean, we haven't even known one another for twenty-four hours yet—but it is true. I do feel safe with you. I guess even my magic felt that."

The implications of what he said bounced through me like happy little bubbles in champagne. I needed to share all my warm and gooey feelings, and what better way than having more amazing, so-good-it-knocks-you-out sex with a beautiful, wonderful man.

And look, Dillon was already naked. Perfect.

Of course, I was wearing a sweaty, cum-encrusted T-shirt, so that was kind of nasty, but Dillon didn't look like he minded.

"So, I guess I have a question," I said. "If you sixty-nine, you don't have to bite my dick for that energy loop thing, right? 'Cause if that's the case, we're never doing that."

Dillon's eyes widened in surprise, then he laughed loud and long. "No. No dick biting. I promise."

"Okay, then." I turned in Dillon's embrace and straddled him. I was sure my smile was big and toothy and goofy looking, but I didn't care because Dillon smiled right back at me. And then we were kissing again and touching. I never wanted this to end.

Chapter Thirteen

DILLON

That afternoon, I held Ash's hand as we approached the Willow Lake Inn. I'd never held anyone's hand before. I hadn't ever wanted to, but there was something about him that made me want to do that and so much more.

We'd spent the whole morning getting hot and sweaty, but it wasn't enough. If we hadn't needed to check in with Van or go to the hardware store, I wasn't sure we would have left the bed, to be honest.

Before we did any of that, though, I needed to feed my little witch. That's why we were here. Ash had suggested going to the Flying Rowan Café where he worked, but I wanted to see the place Rob was so eager to raid.

"I'll show you the inn first, then we'll go to the pub for lunch," Ash suggested as we walked across the gravel parking lot to the massive three-story building.

When I nodded, Ash steered me to the left, which appeared to be the main entrance to the inn. It looked like the pub was attached to the right end of the building and had its own entrance.

To be honest, the place wasn't what I'd expected.

Based on the character of the building, I guessed the place to be at least a hundred years old. Small artistic details were hidden everywhere. The phases of the moon were incorporated into the red brick façade, intricate carvings celebrating the native flora and fauna decorated the thick oak of the main door, and the stone lintel above the door even had a stylized wolf head.

Despite the size and heft of the door, it swung open easily to reveal a large reception room with oversized dark green sofas placed in the middle of the room, which complemented the dark hardwood floors. Everywhere I looked, ornate designs were carved into rich oak beams and panels, all stained in that same dark hue as the floor. The original pack must have treasured their home. Their love for the place was on display in every corner.

To know that the pack in the hills had given up living here to live in the woods in those flimsy shacks was shocking. What could have driven them away from here? What didn't I know?

"Why would they have left this place?"

Ash rolled his shoulders. "I don't know the details, just that it happened around the time that the last alpha died."

Right, I'd forgotten he was fairly new to Willow Lake too.

"I don't really see what anyone would want to steal from here." Ash glanced around the room. "I know Ulric, the old guy who opened the inn, had some kind of magic, but I don't feel anything here, do you?"

I let my hellhound's senses rise. A partial shift didn't give me as much power as a full shift, but it did allow me to see most magic. Nothing revealed itself. So, whatever Rob was after, it wasn't in this part of the building.

"I don't sense anything either," I said.

With nothing to discover here, we didn't linger in the foyer but turned right, toward the hall leading to the pub. I didn't need Ash to tell me where it was. The noise of conversation and laughter was loud enough to direct me to the right door, particularly when the rest of the building seemed eerily quiet. I doubted anyone was even staying at the inn.

When we pushed through the door connecting the inn to the pub, I was struck by the strange medley of magical energies. It was more intense than the general cacophony of magics in the town itself. This wasn't residual energy; this was active.

I scanned the place quickly but didn't see any threats—just a lot of supes of every description all mixing together. The space itself was cozy, although it was obviously a slightly newer addition. The wood detailing wasn't as ornate as the main part of the inn, but it was still finely crafted. Whoever designed it had obviously drawn inspiration from British pubs, with its dark green painted walls, dark beadboard wainscotting, and gleaming brass fittings on the bar. Under the expected aromas of cleaning products, beer, and greasy food was the familiar scent of wolf, as if the original pack's scent would always be embedded into the very foundations of the place.

"Van's here," Ash murmured, nodding toward the hellhound leaning against the bar.

One of Van's eyebrows lifted when he spied us together. Then he nodded, as if to say he'd be with us in a minute.

"Probably checking on the owner," I said.

Ash nodded. "Right. He mentioned that last night, didn't he?"

"At least we won't have to make another stop at the police station now."

Ash's eyes twinkled when he looked up at me. "Eager to get back to the apartment?"

"Well, we do have to change the lock," I said, mustering the most innocent expression I could.

"Of course, that's what you were thinking about," Ash teased. The way his hand squeezed mine suggested he was on board with going back to his place for some privacy too.

Even this early in the day, the place was filled with supes of every description. I tugged Ash closer as he led me deeper into the pub. Given the way he leaned into me, he didn't seem to mind the protective gesture or showing people that we were together, which would be good, because with so many shifters here, there would be no secrets. Every shifter in the place would know we'd had sex. A lot of sex. It didn't matter that we'd showered before leaving the apartment, we stank of one another.

I loved it.

When Ash stifled a yawn, I frowned. Neither of us had gotten much sleep last night. Or this morning. Maybe we should have tried harder to make lunch with the random things he kept in his cupboards, so we could turn in for a nap right after filling our bellies.

But Ash had been determined to get out of the apartment. Very determined. There was a story there, I was sure of it. Had someone tried to keep him safely tucked away at home after he'd been attacked by his boyfriend? Had he been scared to leave his house? I was sure it was one of those things.

I hoped he wasn't forcing himself to leave his apartment now because he was afraid. I didn't think Rob's wolves would return for me. They'd tried and failed. Rob seemed more greedy than vengeful. I doubted he'd send more of his wolves for me. It was too great a risk, with very little reward, especially when there was money to be made at the inn.

Then again, Rob had to know by now I'd talked to the police. Would he even try to carry out the robbery now? I frowned. I doubted the alpha would call it off, especially since he had that magical pendant. And, honestly, he could afford to be a little cocky when he owned such a powerful artifact.

Behind the long bar lined with barstools, which was on the left as we entered, was a youngish man with a mess of brown curly hair. That had to be Jake, the oracle. The one who'd drawn a vision of me running from the wolves. He glanced at us and nodded to Ash. He didn't seem to recognize me, but in his drawing, I'd probably been in my hellhound form.

A woman, who was sitting on one of the barstools in front of him, twisted in her seat to see what had caught the bartender's attention. A pink jacket hung over the back of her chair and her matching pink shirt looked like it was at least two sizes too small for her big breasts. Her eyes lit up when she spied me, and she smoothed her hand over her hair.

I didn't need to scent her to know she was a succubus. It was considered rude to stereotype supes based on their species, but some magical beings had obvious commonalities with the rest of their species. A succubus was one of those supes. They were always interested in sex—it was how they replenished their magic, after all—and often spread their pheromones all over the place hoping to snare a willing participant. This one was looking in the wrong place, though, if she was looking at me. I was smitten with a certain fire mage and not even the most powerful succubus would catch my attention now.

To the right side was a pool table and a few dartboards. Both supes and humans were clustered around the area, seeming to mix comfortably together. Usually, humans shied away from supe hangouts, so I was surprised to see so many.

As if to prove the point about just how bizarre this place was, I spotted a large old troll hunched over a foul looking drink in an alcove close to the pool table. Trolls were usually reclusive and antisocial, and yet here he was, sitting within a few feet of some rowdy shifters and humans.

Willow Lake was strange.

But this had to be the place—the mythical supernatural utopia—I'd overheard the faun talking about. When I'd heard about it, I'd been hopeful. Now that I was here… I wanted to believe I could find a home here. Finally. But was it too good to be true?

If I hadn't wasted a week with the pack in the hills, maybe I'd have figured that out by now.

On the far side of the pub were low wooden tables. Clusters of wooden chairs with padded leather seats encircled them. A semi-private area with glass walls and windows facing the lake, which was across the street, was in the farthest corner.

I followed Ash to one of the round wooden tables. As soon as we were seated, a calico cat leapt onto the table. I didn't need to shift into my hellhound form to feel the power emanating from the deceptively small and fluffy body. This was no ordinary cat, nor was it a typical feline shifter. I didn't know what it was.

"Is this him?" the cat asked. His tail flicked in the air as if to punctuate his question.

Before either of us could answer, the bartender arrived with a small pad of paper and pencil in his hand.

"Hey, Ash," the young brown-haired bartender said. "Do you want your usual?"

"Oh, hi, Jake," Ash said. "I didn't mean for you to have to come get our orders. I was going to come up. But, yeah, my usual would be great. Thanks."

Jake smiled and, honestly, he looked adorable—not as adorable as my little witch, but still cute. If I hadn't met Ash, I might have even been tempted to get to know him a little better, even though there was something fucked up about his magic. I couldn't quite figure out what I was feeling from him, but something wasn't right. I almost wished I could shift and take a good look at him, but there were too many humans around to do that.

"No worries," Jake said, waving away Ash's concern.

Then the guy turned his attention to me. "You must be new to town. I'm Jake. Welcome to the Willow Lake Pub."

His cheeks pinkened as his gaze drifted over the expanse of my shoulders and my bare forearms. The shape of my body was a genetic thing. I didn't have to do much to maintain my muscles, but this wasn't the first time someone had eyed me appreciatively. After all, Ash had done the same thing last night when he'd seen me shift on the road.

Right now, though, Ash didn't look pleased. I grinned as he staked his claim on me by sliding his hand into mine under the table, then lifting our joined hands onto the table. Nothing subtle about my firecracker.

"Jake, this is Dillon. My boyfriend."

My chest warmed at the title. I wanted to be so much more than that, but the title would work for now.

The cat cleared its throat.

"And, Dillon, this is Paws," Ash said, waving toward the cat, who narrowed his eyes at that introduction. Ash rolled his eyes. "Fine. His proper name is Pawington the Third, but he lets us mere mortals call him Paws."

Jake's forehead wrinkled at Ash's introduction of the cat.

"It is nice to meet you finally," Paws said with a sniff.

Jake swallowed hard when Paws spoke, then he averted his eyes. His fingers tightened on the pen and little notebook he carried, like he was pretending not to understand what the cat said. And wasn't that curious? Because people who didn't know about magic, like Jake supposedly didn't, should have heard a cat's meow instead of words.

"What can I get you?" Jake asked quickly. He was barely able to meet my eyes now.

"A Caesar with extra tabasco. Can we look at your menu too?"

As soon as we placed our drink orders, Jake peeled away from the table like it was possessed.

Yeah. I'd bet that Jake knew more than he was letting on. But why would he lie about that? What would he gain by keeping his knowledge of supes a secret?

Ash's phone pinged with a message. He looked at the screen and snorted.

"It's just my friend Jeremy," he said, flashing the message toward me so I could read it.

MyBestestBFF4ever: If vampires only drink blood, what does their pee look like? Because they have to have waste material, right? I suppose I could be convinced that they don't shit because of their liquid diet… but I'm not willing to believe they don't piss.

My witch typed something back, his fingers flying over his screen. I didn't ask what his reply was. Frankly, I didn't know why anyone would want to know about vampire excrement, except maybe a vampire and their doctor.

Ash was just finishing his text when Van came over to our table and sat with us, not waiting for an invitation.

"Two hellhounds in town, hey? Not often you see that." The cat's tail swished back and forth.

"Is that going to be a problem?" And just when I

thought I'd found a place to settle. I mean, I guess I knew on some level that hellhounds didn't settle in packs, but I hadn't sensed Van was territorial of Willow Lake last night when we'd talked.

"No. No problem." Van shook his head, then he looked at the cat. "Quit trying to stir up trouble. We've got enough as it is."

Paws lifted his head as if to say he was above such antics, but the grin on Ash's face suggested the cat was often caught up in the middle of things.

"Speaking of trouble, did you find the other wolf?" I asked.

Van frowned, like he wasn't sure he wanted to answer.

Ash leaned forward. "Did Rob send him away?"

"We followed his trail out of town to a point north of Willow Lake at that old, abandoned gas station."

I didn't know what he was talking about, but Ash nodded like he knew.

Van heaved out a deep breath. "We found him there. Dead."

Ash jolted in surprise. "Dead?"

"I scented other wolves out there too. The scents were all fresh, but I couldn't say for sure if they were there at the same time. The amulet is missing. And, except for the scents, the site didn't offer any leads."

Even if Van didn't have the evidence, it was easy to guess that the wolf had met up with someone from his pack, probably to drop off the magical amulet, and was silenced, permanently. We all sat back and thought about that for a minute. I mean I was happy the threat the wolves posed had been eliminated, but that didn't mean Ash was safe. I prayed that by losing two of his pack—one arrested and one dead— Rob had learned his lesson and wouldn't send any other members of his pack to come after us.

Jake brought our drinks and the menus to the table. We ordered our lunches quickly, then waited for him to leave before resuming our conversation.

"What about the wolf you arrested?"

"He won't talk. Honestly, he stinks of fear. It got worse when we told him about his buddy." Van frowned. "What kind of pack is Robbie running out there?"

It was still weird to hear Van and the others refer to Rob as Robbie.

"He's a shit alpha." I thought back to my week there. "Doesn't understand that loyalty isn't fear-based. I don't get why they all stay there with him, to be honest."

Van clenched his hands, flames danced in his eyes, and his nostrils flared before he slowly relaxed. It looked like it took effort. "Do you know why they left Willow Lake?"

"I don't," I said, then I glanced at Ash.

"I mean I've heard rumors, but I don't know the full story," Ash said with a shrug.

"About twelve years ago or so, the previous alpha and his wife died in a car accident. I tried to investigate, but in the end my superiors ordered me to stop." He clenched his fists again. "They had two sons, Hayden and Robbie. As the oldest heir to the alpha, Hayden was chosen as the successor. Robbie, being a self-important little shit, decided he'd make a better alpha, even though he was young and immature."

I took a sip of my drink, loving the way it burned on the way down, and waited for Van to continue. Some of the other supes in the room were quiet too, as if they were listening in. I wondered if they caught the same subtle insinuation that I had… that Hayden's parents had been murdered.

"Hayden's father had been inviting other supes to move into town for years by that point. He loved the diversity and often held celebrations for all supes, rather than focusing on his pack. Said the Eternal Magic in Willow Lake was healthier and stronger because of it. Hayden wanted to do the same thing. But Robbie got talking in people's ears, whispering about how these people were taking jobs away from the wolves, how they were undermining the pack's authority, how they were corrupting the pack's beliefs, and how all the other supes were just using the pack and looking for weaknesses to exploit so they could take over."

Beside me, Ash shivered.

I whistled and shook my head. "What a bastard."

"Exactly," Van agreed. He took a long draw from his beer before wiping the back of his hand across his mouth.

Van's story was interrupted by a couple of people coming to say hello and then delayed again when Jake delivered our meals to the table. I'd followed Van's suggestion and ordered a spicy burger. One sniff, which burned my nose, told me it was going to be good. My burger was covered in spicy peppers and hot sauce and was so tall it almost toppled when the plate was set in front of me. Perfect. Ash's "blazing inferno" flavored hot wings smelled almost as good as my burger. I'd definitely have to try those next time. We'd taken a few bites when I gestured to Van to continue.

"So… what happened then with Rob?"

"The bastard was cleverer than anyone had given him credit for, that's for sure," Van said after he'd swallowed a bite of his lunch. "Because sure enough, the wolves started believing it. Sure, not all of them, but enough that it was causing problems. Then one of the pack, a young wolf who Robbie's friend had been trying to court, fell for someone else, a raven shifter. Everything came to a head. Robbie spewed a lot of hate to anyone who'd listen. Talked about how the other supes were stealing their mates now and all that." He sucked in a deep breath and eyed the half-eaten burger in his hand, like it held all the answers. "Hayden was never going to kick all the other supes out of town. That just isn't his way, even if a lot of the pack sided with Robbie. In the end, I think Robbie just decided it was easier to leave with his followers instead of challenging Hayden to become alpha. He never would have won a challenge and he knew it. Honestly, if we hadn't been watching so closely, I sometimes wonder if…" Van's words trailed off, but it was easy to figure out what he was going to say.

…if Robbie would have murdered Hayden to take over the pack and Willow Lake.

"Another couple of wolves were found guilty of Carl and Judy's deaths, but… Something about that never sat right with me. Anyway, a bunch of wolves followed Robbie into the woods and have been a thorn in our side ever since. They never do anything that'll draw the SC's attention, but they tend to skirt the law too often for my comfort."

"And Hayden? He said last night there wasn't a

Willow Lake Pack anymore. What happened there? Surely not everyone left with Rob." These were things I needed to know if I was thinking of staying here. I eyed Van as I picked up a slice of banana pepper that'd fallen out of my burger and popped it into my mouth.

Van grimaced before finishing off his pint. "Hayden stepped down as alpha. Said he'd destroyed the pack and he couldn't be trusted to lead. He refused to listen to anyone who said otherwise. Then he sold the packhouse and distributed the money evenly among the people who'd stayed."

"But everyone still treats him like he's their alpha."

"Of course," Van snapped. "He needs to pull his head out of his ass to realize the truth. He's the alpha all right, and his pack is made up of every supe in this town, wolf or not. He's a stubborn asshole, though."

Paws, who'd been quietly cleaning his fur this whole time, looked up then. "If we're done with the history lesson, we need to talk about this attack the bastard has planned."

"Dillon said the attack was scheduled for the new moon, but there is no way to tell if Robbie will change his mind or not," Van said.

"What about the other stuff they've stolen?" I asked.

The cat's ears twitched as his gaze jumped to me. "What other stuff?"

"Rob said they'd done a trial run to test things out."

Paws growled low and menacing. His tail whipped across the table and knocked over Van's empty pint glass. The hellhound grabbed it before it rolled off the table.

"Do you think that's where they got the amulet?" Ash

slipped his hand in mine again and squeezed, and I knew he was remembering last night's attack.

"What amulet?" Paws glared at Van. "I should have been told about this."

"The amulet made it so we couldn't hear, taste or smell anything."

"That sounds like something from Ulric's collection." Paws growled again, then he leapt off the table. He glanced over his shoulder as he toddled away from us. "Well, come on. Don't dawdle."

Luckily we'd all finished eating. We downed our drinks. As we passed by the bar, I tossed some bills on the counter for Jake. "Thanks."

Paws led us back to the inn, through the foyer and up the stairs. The scent of wolves was stronger here. When this building was still a pack house, these rooms had probably been used as the wolves' private quarters. The hallway was clean, but the paint and fittings were showing their age. The whole place could use a refresh. The light overhead hummed and cast a yellow glow over us as we followed the cat.

Paws stopped in front of a door at the end of the corridor and looked at Van expectantly. The hellhound stepped forward and opened the door to reveal a room that looked like it could be used as a movie set about a crazy wizard. The large space was in the shape of an octagon with windows facing both the lake to the south and the woods to the west and northwest. The furnishings were arranged in small clusters, presumably to encourage intimate conversations. Tucked against the wall were cabinets of every shape and size, filled with curious-looking artifacts. I stepped inside to get a closer look. Magical energy enveloped me and made me freeze. Why was all this magic just lying out here for anyone to grab?

"Why wasn't the door locked?" I asked.

Ash stepped in behind me. I knew he felt the magic too when he shivered.

"When Ulric was alive, he used a theft-deterrent magic on the cabinets. Jake doesn't know how to do that. Hell, the kid probably doesn't even know wards exist or what they do." Paws hopped up on a worn, old fashioned looking loveseat with faded black and white stripes. "We really gotta educate him... I'm open this coming Tuesday."

"No way." Ash scoffed. "That's your day on the pool."

I didn't know what they were talking about, but I could tell they weren't being serious.

"He might have a point, though," I said as I looked at the collection inside the nearest case. I didn't see obvious gaps in the arrangement, and I didn't think the people Rob sent would be smart enough to rearrange the display to hide if they'd taken anything from it. "Jake needs to be aware of what's going on, so he can implement better protection."

Van scrubbed his hand over his face. "We've tried. It's like the kid's eyes go blank and he can't hear us anytime we try talking to him about the Eternal Magic."

"Is anything missing? It feels like the wards are still active," Ash said as he brushed his finger over one of the locks, the only barrier between us and what appeared to be freaky toys inspired by nightmares. I leaned in for a better look.

No. These weren't macabre toys, they were small mascots. The longer I stared at the creepy little dolls, the more they seemed familiar, unlocking long forgotten memories. Right. That was it. Some people in the old countries used them to ward off evil. So, even though the things looked sinister, they had a non-threatening feeling about them. The magic was meant to protect, not harm.

"Come over here, kid," Paws said.

Showing more trust in the powerful creature than what I was comfortable with, Ash crossed the room to Paws.

"Come closer…"

Ash bent over and Paws leapt onto his shoulder. Ash cried out in surprise, and I bolted to his side. I scented blood in the air. The bastard cat had scratched my witch. I growled and reached for the furry little menace, ready to fling him off my mage's body. Paws hit my hand with his paw, claws out, and hissed at me.

"Hey," Ash shouted at the cat. "Watch your claws. This is cashmere." Then he looked at me. "It's okay. He just surprised me."

"Now, show me what's over there," Paws commanded, waving his paw toward another nearby cabinet.

Ash rolled his eyes. "Couldn't you have just asked to be picked up?"

"I am not a baby to be cradled in someone's arms."

"And I'm not your personal transport either."

Paws huffed but wrapped himself around Ash's neck. When he was settled, he flicked his tail. "Well, go on. What are you waiting for?"

Ash shook his head but ferried the cat around to look inside each of the cabinets. I followed behind. No doubt about it, the objects on display all had magical properties, but nothing felt overly menacing or dark. Maybe the old man who'd owned and displayed these artifacts wasn't as irresponsible as it'd first appeared.

"Well?" Van asked.

"Nothing's missing." Paws sounded as confused as I felt.

"Is there another room like this?"

Paws shook his head and twitched his tail. "Ulric's suite has stuff too, but the ward is still secure on that room. I check it every day. Nothing's changed."

"Well, maybe they stole non-magical things, like silverware from the kitchen, when they broke in. It's possible the amulet came from somewhere else," Ash suggested.

"Maybe…" I said, but I didn't believe it. By the looks on everyone else's faces, they didn't believe it either. Rob wouldn't have wanted his people to miss the opportunity to grab something magically valuable.

"So what's the plan?" Ash asked.

I suspected if Van didn't have a plan, Ash would come up with something on his own. He was still shooting sparks from his fingers whenever he thought too long on the wolves who'd broken into his apartment last night.

"The new moon is tomorrow night," Van said. "We'll set up a patrol starting tonight and keep it up for the next couple of nights. If nothing happens, we'll reevaluate."

Chapter Fourteen

ASH

After lunch, we returned to my apartment to rest. In my mind, I put quotation marks around *rest*, because sleep really wasn't on my mind, if you know what I mean.

We could nap later—much, much later—and still be in good shape for tonight. Van had warned it'd likely be a late night, so I didn't want to be tired going into it. I wouldn't be much help if I had to trundle off to a corner for a snooze.

If nothing happened tonight, I was going to have to talk to my boss about my shifts at the restaurant over the next few days. Parker liked having me in charge of pizza on the weekends, often saying no one else could maintain the fire in the pizza oven like I could. But with the wolf pack circling, making pizza wasn't my highest priority.

Unfortunately, Parker was one of the humans in town and didn't know about magic, which meant he wouldn't know about the wolf threat. I'd have to come up with a different excuse, something he'd buy that wouldn't mess up my relationship with him because I liked Parker, and I liked my job.

As soon as the door shut behind us, I pulled on Dillon's hand, determined to get us to the bedroom as quickly as possible. Dillon didn't budge.

"Hold on, firecracker," he said. I glanced to the bedroom, then back at him. It was right there. Just a few steps away.

"Why?" I whined.

"We need to get these locks installed first." He lifted the shopping bag he was carrying. The contents clanged together.

"Fine." I huffed. "But we only need to do one, right?"

"We're doing all three."

"I still think three is a crazy number of locks to install on one door." Although I could see his point. The one lock on my doorknob had done nothing to keep the wolves out last night. But now I'd have my original deadbolt and three new locks. It seemed like overkill.

"Where is your toolkit?"

I huffed and went to get a kitchen chair to use as a stool. Being shorter than the average man sucked. I brought it back to the closet beside my front door and dug out my meager selection of tools from the back of the top shelf. Calling it a toolkit was a bit of an exaggeration when it wasn't much more than a canvas bag containing three random screwdrivers, a hammer, and a rusty set of pliers.

Luckily, Dillon managed to work with the few tools I had. When we finished, I eyed the locks skeptically. There was no way I was getting my full security deposit back with that many new holes in my door and door frame. But I couldn't deny I did feel safer. Of course, that could have been because I was now locked inside my apartment with a big, sexy hellhound.

I was shoving my toolkit back onto the shelf in my front closet when my phone rang.

I knew by the *Bewitched* theme song it was my mother. The song was old school, and I hadn't even watched any of the episodes, but the ringtone made me smile whenever she called and that was a good thing. If I wasn't smiling when I talked to her, she'd decide something was wrong and make a special trip to Willow Lake to check on me.

For the tiniest moment, I contemplated ignoring her call but that would make her panic. The last thing I needed was for her to call the police station to get them to do a wellness check. Ask me how I knew she'd do that.

I jumped down from the chair and swiped to answer.

"Hi, Mom," I said, forcing an upbeat enthusiasm into my words.

I was greeted with silence for half a second, then, "What's wrong?"

Spells and curses, now I'd fucked up. "Nothing's wrong."

"You don't sound right, honey," she said. "What happened?"

I could already hear the jingle of her keys and knew she'd grabbed them off the hook by her front door.

"Mom, seriously, I'm fine."

"I can be there in a jiffy," she said.

The sound of the front door closing punctuated her words. The last thing I needed was for her to drive two hours because she didn't like the way I answered the phone.

"Stop," I said forcefully.

Everything went silent on her end. Dillon, who wore a worried look on his face, froze too. He'd been returning the kitchen chair I'd been standing on to reach into the closet. His hands tightened on the back of the chair.

"I have plans," I said. "I won't be here if you come today."

"What plans?"

"Mom, I'm an adult. I can make plans without needing to tell you about them. Do you ask Birch for details about his plans?"

"Birch doesn't make plans, honey, he hooks up with people. Is that what you're talking about? Sex?" I swear I heard her clap her hands. "Are you having sex again? Oh, honey, I'm so proud of you."

"Please stop talking." I groaned and flopped down on my sofa.

"Who is this guy, Ashton? What's his name? Is he a supe? How long have you known him?"

Good grief. "Mom, please…"

She sighed. "You know you don't have a good history, honey. I think we'd both feel better if you told me about him. And send me a picture of him at the start of your date. And text me whatever details he tells you about himself."

I glanced at Dillon who'd joined me on the couch, expecting him to roll his eyes at her ridiculousness. I figured, with his shifter senses, he could hear everything she said. Instead of being exasperated like I was, he was nodding like he agreed with her.

"I'm okay with that, Ash," he whispered, "if it'll make her feel better. I'm glad you have someone looking out for you."

"What was that?" my mom asked.

"That was Dillon—"

"He's there? Right now?" My mom squealed—literally squealed—like the wonky wheel on the cart I always managed to grab at the grocery store. "You didn't tell me he was in your apartment. It must be serious. I'm so proud of you, firebug. So proud of you for putting yourself out there again. I'm going to hang up and call you back real quick for a video call."

Before I could stop her, she'd already disconnected. Sometimes I wished Birch and I had never shown her how to make a video call. Not even a second later, the request for a video call came in. Reluctantly, I accepted it.

"Hi again, honey." She waved with one hand as she smoothed her hair into place with the other. Fixing her hair never worked. Her air magic always made her hair stand up and go all over the place; today was no different.

"Hi, Mom," I said.

"Introduce me to your guy."

I glanced at Dillon. I'd already introduced him at the pub as my boyfriend and he didn't seem to mind, so I guess he was *my guy*. But having him meet my mother, even if it was just through video, was next level. He had no idea what was coming, but he was already reaching for the phone.

"Oh, you're a big one, aren't you?" She hummed appreciatively as soon as he swung the camera toward his face.

"Mom!"

"Well, he is, honey. Look at him. I mean, I knew you liked them big all over, but... He's one big mountain of a man. And so good looking too."

Did my mom just call me a size queen? I wanted to crawl under the sofa.

Dillon's cheeks darkened. Aw... was he blushing? "Hello, Mrs. Avery. It's nice to meet you."

"Oh, and so polite. I like him."

"He's sitting right here, Mom. He can hear everything you're saying."

"Then he should know I'm recording this conversation and will be googling him as soon as I'm off the phone."

Dillon laughed and glanced at me. "I like her too."

My mom grinned.

"What would you like to know, ma'am?"

As his words—and the fact that he hadn't run for the door—sank in, a warm fluttering feeling filled my chest. Chris would never have agreed to this. He'd never have encouraged her stalking tendencies. Of course, before Chris, she'd never been as insanely protective of me as she was now.

I sat on the edge of the sofa, poised to grab my phone as soon as my mother became too much for him to handle. She could be intense. I suspected even Van could learn a thing or two about interrogation from my mother. But as Dillon answered her many, *many* questions, he didn't get annoyed or tense or short with her.

She posed serious questions and some off-the-wall ones too, and he answered everything without hesitation.

He laughed. And she laughed. And, as the conversation continued, my tension eased.

Dillon pulled me close, wrapping his arm around me until I curled up with my head on his shoulder. I loved how his body heat wrapped around me. I almost didn't need to wear sweaters when he was close.

"Aw… You two look so good together." Mom had her hands clasped in front of her chest like she was looking at the most precious thing in the world. "I'm looking forward to meeting you soon, Dillon."

"Me too, Mrs. Avery."

"Oh, please call me Nerine."

"Of course, Nerine," he said.

"Excellent. Ash honey, I'll call you in a couple of days." And then she was gone.

Dillon put my phone on the side table.

"I'm sorry about that," I said.

"About what?" He sounded confused.

"My mom. The interrogation. All of that." I waved toward my phone.

Dillon brushed a kiss to the top of my head. "I like that she's protective of you. I can see how it probably feels overwhelming for you, but I didn't mind answering her questions and easing some of her worry. What happened in your past was probably hard on both of you. I'm angry it happened and that you both are so cautious now because of it, but if I can ease any of those worries, I'm happy to do it."

"Thank you." I turned my face up to his. "I know things weren't easy for her or my brother after the attack. I was in the hospital for a long time and then in physio. My recovery was longer than anticipated because my magic was so damaged. But one of the reasons I moved to Willow Lake was because they kept coddling me. I needed to prove to them both—and myself, I guess—that I was still the same person I was before... or, well, not the same exactly, but that I didn't have to be thrown in a room full of packing peanuts and just brought out on special occasions."

Dillon squeezed me tight to his chest.

"That didn't sound very appreciative, did it? I mean I love them. I know what they did was because they love me too. But I couldn't hide in my mother's house or cower behind my brother for the rest of my life. They hated that I moved away, but living like that... I just couldn't stay there any longer."

"I know, little witch. And I know I want to protect you too. Not because of your past, but because you are special to me. So please, if you feel like I'm too clingy or controlling, talk to me about it. I don't want to change you or stop you from living your life. But I'm not sure my intentions will always come across that way."

"I'm not helpless. Even if my magic is wonky."

"I know. I never thought you were."

Okay. That was good. I yawned and snuggled closer.

"We should go to the bedroom."

"Oh?" I perked up.

"To sleep," he clarified. "I suspect we're going to have a long night."

"Fine."

I dragged him to the bed, determined to change his

mind. Yes, I was tired, but hello? There was a sexy hell-hound in my bed. Who wanted sleep?

I yawned again.

Damn it.

Me, apparently. I wanted sleep.

Within minutes of curling up against Dillon's side, I couldn't quit yawning, nor could I keep my eyes open.

Okay. Fine. I'd sleep. But when we woke up, nothing was going to stop me from getting to know my hellhound better. Every inch of him.

·

Chapter Fifteen

DILLON

I knew Ash was awake by the way the little tease rubbed his ass against my cock. We'd stripped down to our T-shirts and underwear before climbing into bed for our nap and that thin fabric was doing nothing to hide my erection.

We'd returned to my favorite position of me being the big spoon and him the little one. Even in my sleep, it seemed, I was compelled to protect him. But right now, I needed him to stop moving before he made me come from his wiggling, so I tightened my hold on him. I was careful to keep my hand on top of his T-shirt, even though I ached to reach under and feel his warm skin.

"I could get used to waking up with you." He let out a contented sigh and snuggled even closer. The scent of his growing arousal was intoxicating.

"Hmmm…" I was too distracted to form words. I pressed my face into his dark hair and breathed him in. Fuck. He smelled so good. I wanted to roll in his scent and coat myself in it. Then everyone, from those pissant wolves in the hills to the Chief of Police, would know I was his.

I rolled my hips against his ass, unable to stop myself now that he'd woken my need for him. His breath caught and he arched in my arms, as if seeking more. He reached around and gripped my hip to hold me tight against him.

"Are you sure you're up for this already?" I murmured into his hair.

I wasn't being boastful, but my cock was big. I knew it was. Everyone who'd ever seen it, Ash included, had confirmed it. After this morning, I figured he might be a little tender, particularly if he hadn't been with anyone for a while. I refused to hurt my little witch, even if his body was begging for my cock right now.

"Were you…" He swallowed and twisted in my arms so he could face me. His pale gray-green gaze caught on mine. "Were you serious about bottoming?"

My heart beats quickened, and I nodded. Most people looked at me and decided I was only good for one thing. Apparently being held down, topped roughly, and thoroughly dominated by a big guy was a common fantasy, because that's what most of my past hookups wanted. It meant I didn't have the chance to bottom very often.

"I'd love to feel you inside me," I confirmed.

His eyes lit up with the red of his magic as he pushed me onto my back. My already hard cock stiffened even more as he crawled over me and straddled my hips.

"I'm going to make you feel so good," he promised. Then he leaned forward and kissed me. His hands pushed at my shirt to reveal my stomach and chest. "I love the feel of you."

My hands clenched on his hips, aching to explore him too, but I wasn't going to have a repeat of earlier. I could keep my hands under control if it meant Ash felt happy and safe. The witch sat back, so his ass pressed against my cock. Eager to feel more of him, my hips rocked against him. He stared at me for a long moment, then he reached for the bottom of his shirt. I swallowed hard and gripped his hips even tighter.

"Are you sure, Ash?" My voice was thick with all the emotions I couldn't contain. "Because I can wait, baby."

He stared straight into my eyes as he pulled his shirt higher until it covered his face and left his chest bare. He stayed that way for a long moment, as if hiding behind the fabric was his one last defense. I thought about not looking, but he was sharing this part of himself with me. He was trusting me with this. The least I could do was honor that trust by looking.

I hadn't seen many magical injuries, and most shifters, myself included, healed quickly and without scarring, so what I saw was shocking. I wasn't sure if it was the nature of the attack Ash had suffered or if it was because he was a mage, but the scars were still vivid streaks over his chest, a stark contrast to the pale, smooth skin covering the rest of his body.

He'd said the attack had focused on his magical core, which apparently lived close to his chest based on the one-inch sized patch of angry pink skin over his sternum. That small bit of mottled scarred skin was at the epicenter of all the other scars on his chest. Rolls of white corded scar tissue radiated out in eight directions, stretching out over his entire torso. The scars were too evenly distributed to be coincidental. I would bet anything that they had aligned with the cardinal and ordinal directions during the attack.

Fuck.

If the bastard had drawn power from all points, what did it mean? Had the guy possessed so very little magic that he'd needed the boost? Or had he needed the extra power because wielding magic in such an unnatural way would have been a struggle? Either way, he had to have practiced some dark fucked up magic to sustain an attack like that long enough to cause this kind of damage.

I wanted to hunt down Ash's ex in his prison cell and do what hellhounds did best—destroy him in the name of justice. Questions surged through me, but Ash had already told me his story; he didn't need me badgering him about it. I bit down on my tongue before I could voice them, welcoming the taste of blood in my mouth. The pain grounded me, helping me focus on this moment again, but the questions didn't stop. I bit down harder on my tongue, refusing to release them.

Ash didn't need my questions. He would think I was questioning his strength as a mage, even if I wasn't. He was strong, probably one of the strongest mages I'd ever encountered. I hated that he didn't believe me when I'd told him that. At least not yet.

Then the shirt was off. Ash had closed his eyes, still hiding.

"Does it hurt?" I let the only important question slip free.

"Itches from time to time," he whispered as he shook

his head. "And... and... some nights I wake up screaming... I guess I should warn you about that if we sleep
together again. Although it happens less frequently now
than before. It's just part of my recovery. Or something
like that. I worked through most of that with a therapist.
But the scars themselves don't really hurt. Not
anymore..."

I couldn't hold back any longer. I needed to hold him,
kiss him, show him how thankful I was that he'd survived.
When my lips brushed his, he gasped in surprise and
reached out to grab me. He pulled back a bit, his eyes
open now.

"Are you sure they don't bother you?"

"Absolutely they bother me, but not in the way you are
thinking. I want to rip your ex apart with my bare hands
and soak the earth with his blood."

His eyebrows shot up his forehead.

"But seeing your scars doesn't make me want you any
less." In fact, my every instinct was screaming at me to
never let him go. To protect him at all costs. To worship
him until he believed he was worthy of being worshiped.
And then to keep doing it over and over again for the rest
of our lives.

He shivered as he leaned into my embrace. He inhaled
and exhaled deeply as he settled against me. We stayed
that way for a long, long time before he started wiggling
against me again.

When he sat up, rubbing his ass against my cock, the
furrows of worry and discomfort were gone. I doubted I'd
chased away all his anxieties with one hug, but the fear in
his eyes was slowly being replaced by mischief as his

hands drifted down my chest. He seemed intent on finding all my ticklish spots and making me squirm.

"I think I like having you under me," he said as he rotated his hips and rubbed against me in a way that was way too seductive for such a little movement. When he waggled his eyebrows and grinned at me salaciously, he surprised a laugh out of me. I knew he was trying to lighten the mood from our conversation about his scars, but I also knew I liked being under him too.

"Stay still," he commanded, and I had no problem obeying.

At least I had no problem obeying until he proceeded to edge me like a fucking expert. His hands peeled off my clothes and cast them over the side of the bed, then he set about kissing and caressing every inch of me—from my pinkie to my toes—everything except my cock. He swatted my hand when I reached for myself. I groaned, closed my eyes, and prayed I had the strength to get through this sweet torture.

"I said stay still," he corrected me and, fuck if that didn't make my cock drool even more.

"Ash—"

Whatever I was about to do—beg, bargain, negotiate— was lost as he took me into his hot, wet mouth. My eyes shot open, and my hips bucked.

"Fuck…" I groaned as I grappled for control.

He hummed, as if pleased with my reaction. The vibration rolled right over my cock and down into my balls. Then he set out to destroy whatever control I still had.

"Ash…" I warned, seconds away from exploding.

His mouth and hands disappeared.

"No… Please…" I'd never begged anyone before, but I didn't care if Ash knew the control he had over me.

He grinned at me. His swollen lips were wet and red. His fast, panting breaths sounded harsh in the quiet of the bedroom. And judging by the look in his magic-lit eyes, he was ready to devour me. My dick twitched and I fought the urge to come just from him looking at me like that.

"Roll over," he said in a husky voice.

A sigh of relief escaped me as I did as he asked. I liked looking at him and watching him, but I hadn't been looking forward to trying to roll my bulk into a ball to show him my ass. I expected him to grab his industrial sized bottle of lube and start prepping me.

I was so ready for this. My hellhound was too. My body was already heated, and smoke curled out of my nose. My little witch had different ideas, though, and instead of going straight for my ass, he dropped kisses and little kitten licks along the back of my neck.

I shivered. A low growl that almost sounded like a purr —except my hellhound would never, ever purr—rumbled through my chest.

"You smell so good," he whispered against my skin, and I could hear the smile in his voice.

He worked his way all over my body—tasting and kissing my back and along the length of my spine all the way to my ass until I was ready to explode. I moaned and rocked my hips, so my cock rubbed against the soft sheets. He huffed out a little laugh but kept doing what he was doing until I thought I was going to explode. Finally, I heard the snick of the lube opening, followed by a squelching sound.

"Thank fuck," I groaned.

I spread my legs and arched so my ass was in the air.

His touch was soft and tentative as his finger swept over my hole.

"Yes," I hissed.

"You like that, huh?" he teased. The little brat.

I twisted to look over my shoulder at him. His face was serious as he concentrated on his task.

"Have you done this before?"

A blush erupted over his cheeks. "Uh… no… not topping. But I know how to. And I know how to make it feel good."

Then he slipped the tip of his finger inside. I closed my eyes and dropped my head back to the pillow, then I rose on my knees to have more leverage as I rolled my hips and sought more of him.

"You can go faster," I gritted out between clenched teeth as he slowly dragged his finger in and out. In and out. At this rate I was going to come long before he got around to fucking me. "You won't hurt me."

Shifters healed fast. Even if I wasn't completely prepped, I'd be okay.

"I'm in charge right now," he said, as he slapped my ass. "And I'm going to make you feel so good."

"I already feel good," I forced out as he slipped in another finger.

Then he rotated his fingers—there had to be more than two now—and brushed over that magic spot deep inside me. I moaned and pushed into his touch as he swept his other hand over my balls and down to my aching cock. Fuck. He was trying to kill me. I sucked in a breath and tried to count backwards from one hundred. Anything to stop from losing it.

"Ngh… Fuck, baby… You're killing me." I panted as he teased me. "Don't want to come until you're inside me. Need you."

Ash pulled his fingers away as he kissed my back, then I felt his legs brush against mine.

"Open your legs wider," he said as he patted the insides of my thighs. "Your ass is too high for me."

I slid my knees over the sheets until he grunted in approval. As soon as I was braced on my hands and knees, he was right behind me. The sweet pressure as he pushed inside me was pure bliss. My whole body shook. He stopped part way. No fucking way. I wanted all of him. So I rocked back on my knees until he was all the way in. His hips against my ass, his balls against mine.

"So good," I moaned.

He gripped my hips but didn't move. But this time I didn't do anything, savoring the way he filled me up. His magic stirred through the air a moment before he shifted his hips. His panting breath fell over my heated skin like he was fanning the flames inside my blood. My fingers curled into the sheets under me as my hellhound pushed against my skin.

No.

I couldn't let my hellhound any closer. He was an unpredictable bastard with only one thought: to claim Ash in every possible way. I fought to rein in my beast as the witch rolled his hips. So fucking good. He felt made to be inside me, over me, with me. I wondered if this was what being home felt like. Whatever this was, I never wanted it to end.

Ash's fire magic flared around us in crimson, and my hellhound's bright golden orange surged to the surface to meet it. Until meeting Ash, I'd never seen a manifestation of my hellhound's magic while I was in my human form. Not like this. It was as if the magic inside me was drawn out by his. Any word I could think of—beautiful, breathtaking, amazing—was inadequate to describe the way our magics wove together. It was stunning the first time it'd happened, and now it was even more intense and awe-inspiring.

My magic's fire rolled along my fingers as I clenched the soft sheets. Smoke curled out of my mouth and nose. And there was nothing I could do to stop any of it. My beast's magic wanted to play with Ash's.

Each frantic stroke of his body into mine stoked the heat between us. Our bodies slapped against one another in a frenzied rhythm as we chased our pleasure.

With a hoarse cry, he came. His grip on me tightened and his body tensed. Feeling the heat of his release filling me was enough to send me over too. Magical fireworks exploded around us, tantalizing my senses. I reached back and grabbed his hands, needing to feel more of him as pleasure obliterated everything else.

Would sex be like this every time with Ash? Because, fuck…

Chapter Sixteen

ASH

When we returned to the pub that evening, the place was bustling with activity. I marveled at everyone's energy. Dozing in the middle of the day had paradoxically made me more tired. Or maybe that last round of crazy sex had left me relaxed and sleepy.

As if to show everyone exactly how tired I was, my mouth stretched wide in a jaw cracking yawn.

"Maybe you should go home?" Dillon suggested. "Turn in early tonight."

I rubbed my eyes, then frowned at him. "Absolutely not. This is my town, and these are my friends. I'm going to do my part to show those stupid werewolves they don't belong here."

"Yeah." Dillon frowned right back at me. "I figured that would be your response, but I thought I'd try."

A sharp shrill whistle pierced through the rumble of conversations, silencing everyone.

"All right, everyone. Listen up," Van said in a loud voice that carried to every corner of the pub. "Sally has taken Jake into the city for the weekend, so we don't have to worry about him. He thinks there is a gas leak at the inn. Even then, he didn't want to go, but Sally and Alice finally managed to convince him to take a break while it is being fixed. He insisted on taking Paws."

"Man, I wish I'd been here to see Jake manhandle Paws into a cat-carrier," I whispered to Dillon. I'd have paid to watch that.

Around us, a few people groaned at the news. A few others exchanged money, whispering about the bet. Dillon looked confused. Right. I guess I hadn't told him yet about the bet on when Jake would discover magic. With Jake in the city for the night, it looked like there was still time for Dillon to enter his own guess.

"The sun sets at about 9:30 tonight," Van continued, "so we have a few hours to get organized. We're going to divide people into tasks. Some of you will be running the perimeter. Others will be hunkering down inside the inn itself in case anyone gets through. Our goal is to contain any intruders. We don't want anyone killed. Got it?"

Old Thom, the grizzly old troll, harrumphed at that from his regular corner in the darkest part of the pub. I wondered if he had been here the entire day.

"Okay. Anyone who wants to run the perimeter, go talk to Hayden. Everyone else, you get me."

I nudged Dillon. "You should go talk to Hayden."

"I'm going wherever you are, little firecracker."

I rolled my eyes, but I really wanted to do a happy dance. I hadn't been looking forward to being away from him for the night; I couldn't get enough of him. "Then I guess we're with Van, because I don't think I'd be much good on patrol."

"Good." Dillon nodded like he approved. "With any luck, the wolves will be stopped well before they get anywhere near here."

I agreed with him. I had no desire to put myself in harm's way when I still didn't trust my magic. Sure, Dillon had said my magic was strong, but I hadn't seen any evidence of that. Even during the wolf attack at my apartment, all my magic did was light up my fingers like sparklers on a birthday cake. I wondered if that's why Dillon had started calling me firecracker.

"Don't worry," Dillon said, obviously picking up on my anxiety. "If by some fluke the wolves make it here, I'll protect you. No one is ever going to harm you. Never again. I will stop anyone who tries. Permanently."

I grinned up at him as I rose on my toes and kissed him soundly. I shouldn't encourage his desire to kill and maim for me, but how could I resist him when he got all growly and protective?

I looked at the other supes clustered around Van. Most of the bird and large predatory shifters, including the sweet couple, Mercer and Oak, who ran the local gift shop Sparkle and Spice, followed Hayden outside to discuss patrol duty. Those of us who remained inside were an odd mix.

Muriel Rivers, a motherly cat shifter, was hissing at Old Thom. Her husband and several of her sons just stood by and watched. It really was strange to see a supe family with so many children. I'd only seen it happen in Willow

Lake. Before I became too philosophical, I saw Simon, one of Muriel's sons, slowly inch away from his family. He looked ready to shift and hide under a chair until this was all over. Dot, Van's deputy, was dashing back and forth with cardboard boxes filled with who knew what, supplies presumably. Weston the merman was eying the last of the group tagging along behind Hayden like he wanted to be with them, so I doubted he'd stay in here long. Alice the part time bartender, who was also a brownie, was chatting with Henrietta and Gary, the couple who owned the bakery. Earlier I had overheard them asking about Sally the succubus and, based on the way their tentacles drooped and the glow in their eyes dimmed when they'd heard she'd gone to the city with Jake, they were disappointed she wasn't here.

There were more too, many of whom looked familiar but who I'd never met. They seemed flustered at the idea of facing off against wolves, but they'd still shown up, so that was impressive. More surprising was that although I hadn't been able to glean more than a fleeting impression of other people's magic in years, my senses tingled as I neared them. It took a minute to register that sensation as my magic.

As soon as I acknowledged my magic, the energy in it grew. Suddenly, I could tell the group closest to us were smaller shifters like mice or gophers or something. My mouth fell open as I let my magic poke at them again.

It was really working.

It'd been so long since I'd felt anything like it.

This didn't mean my magic was fixed or that it was strong like Dillon thought, but it was something.

Something spectacular. I wanted to buy a round for everyone to celebrate but drinking before potentially being attacked by asshole werewolves didn't seem like the smartest thing.

After this was over? I was totally treating everyone to a round.

The timing of my sudden magical resurgence had me wondering, though. Was my magic coming back because I'd met Dillon? Or had it returned ages ago and I'd been ignoring it?

I doubted I'd ever know the answer to that, but I suspected meeting Dillon was part of it. I just wish I understood why or how.

Van counted everyone and then nodded to himself. When he cleared his throat, everyone turned to listen. "Okay, so here's what's going to happen. We have enough people to have someone stationed at every door and window on the main floor. That's good. I will assign you each a spot. If you sense anything out of the ordinary when you're at your post, you're going to call for me. I'll be circulating through all the rooms on this floor. I will hear you. Don't worry about being noisy. That might scare the wolves off as well as anything else. Any questions?"

I wasn't surprised when the questions started. Van answered them calmly and thoroughly, all things considered. You know that saying about no question being a stupid question? I wasn't so sure about that. How Van didn't roll his eyes and answer a few of the questions with a heavy dose of sarcasm, I'll never know.

After all, did people actually think the sheriff would issue them firearms without them joining the police or, you know, having any training? Or what about the mouse shifter—Dillon had confirmed my suspicion about what kind of shifter the woman was—who asked what would happen if they had to pee. Should they just go on the floor?

Ewww.

And the answer was, of course, an emphatic "No, tell your neighbor you are leaving your position, and then go use the toilet like a civilized fucking person." Okay, so Van maybe hadn't said it exactly like that, but really?

After everyone had been assigned a door or a window and the large shifters had finished up planning their patrol routes and procedures, a truckload of pizzas from the Flying Rowan Café was delivered.

As soon as Parker, my very human boss, entered the pub with an armful of pizzas, Levi bolted over to him and relieved him of half the boxes. Parker eyed everyone curiously as he followed the big minotaur into the pub. I waved at him when he spotted me.

"I didn't know there was an event at the pub today," he said as they set the pizzas on a nearby table.

Before I could say anything, Levi tried to redirect his attention by asking a question. "Are there more to unload?"

"Is there something going on?" Parker asked.

"No. Nothing," Levi said quickly. Too quickly.

Parker narrowed his eyes at Levi. Yeah, I wouldn't have believed the minotaur either.

"Are there more pizzas to bring in?" Levi asked again.

Parker's lips flattened, but he nodded and waved at Levi to follow him. I didn't know what Levi told Parker when they were outside, but when they returned Parker was obviously irritated and Levi's cheeks were a rosy color. They didn't speak to one another as Hayden paid for the pizzas.

When Parker left, Levi rubbed his cheeks and sank into one of the chairs. Hopefully Parker wasn't too mad. We probably should have arranged for someone to pick the pizzas up. No one wanted the humans to get suspicious.

I nudged Dillon. "Why did Hayden pay for everything?"

He shrugged as we watched Hayden distribute the pizzas around the room.

"He does things like that all the time," I continued. "I can't figure out why he can't accept he's the alpha here. I mean he acts like it."

"Does it matter?" Dillon asked.

"He should just officially adopt the title and file the pack's registration with the Supernatural Council."

"What a person does is more important than what their title is."

I supposed that was true, but it still bugged me. Still, I had enough of my own problems; I doubted I could solve Hayden's too. I shut my mouth, though, because Hayden was coming over to our table now.

The pizzas weren't as good as the ones I made, but I wasn't going to complain. They were a little limp but still tasty. Whoever was cooking pizzas today hadn't gotten the oven hot enough before putting them in.

I'd just finished my first slice when my phone announced a text.

MyBestestBFF4ever: If you were a witch, what

kind of familiar would you want? I think I'd
choose a raccoon. Or maybe a squirrel.

Me: Tough one. Maybe a monkey? Then they
could climb up to the top of the cupboards and
get stuff I can't reach.

Like today, when I'd had to get that chair so I could
reach the top shelf in my closet for the tools. But why
would Jer want a raccoon or a squirrel? Although, I could
totally see him with either of those so maybe it made
sense.

I wanted to tell him mages didn't have familiars, but I
couldn't. And, now that he'd asked, I wondered where that
myth had originated. Did witches historically keep
companion animals for security reasons? I could see where
either a large or yappy dog would be useful when you
didn't know if your neighbors would suddenly show up at
your doorstep with torches and pitchforks. After all, people
could turn on other people over the stupidest things. Just
like that stupid werewolf alpha in the hills. Why did he
have to turn his greedy eyes in this direction?

As everyone ate, conversations were subdued.
Anticipation and worry clung to the air, and I was happy I
didn't have to smell everyone's fear like the shifters did. I
doubted it smelled very good.

"Do you think we're overreacting?" I asked Dillon as I
debated eating another slice.

"What do you mean?"

"We're trying to stop someone from stealing things. It
didn't sound like they planned to burn the place down or
kill Jake in his sleep or anything like that. It isn't like we

are going to war. Everyone is so somber, though. It's weird. I'm not saying Rob shouldn't be stopped, because obviously he can't be allowed to do things like this. Or is it because everyone thinks he killed his parents and got away with it? Do they think he was planning to do more than just steal?" I looked at Dillon. A cold chill swept over me as I remembered what happened to the guy who'd attacked us last night, and I rubbed my chest absently. "Do you think the wolves would have hurt Jake?"

"I don't know," Dillon said. "I hope not."

I hadn't thought Chris would try to kill me either. Maybe everyone was right to be worried. Things escalated quickly if no one was there to stop them. Greed, whether for magic or magical objects, could make people crazy. And if these wolves got away with stealing, what would they try to get away with next time?

I shivered.

"What is it?" Dillon squeezed my leg gently. The hell-hound hadn't stopped touching me since we'd arrived, and I was thoroughly enjoying it.

"Nothing specific really." I shook my head. "I just don't want this situation to spiral out of control. You don't think it will, do you?"

"I hope not," he said again as he pressed a kiss to my temple.

"I don't get why people have to be so nasty to one another. Rob is greedy. He values money and his own personal wishes over everyone and everything. I wish people like him didn't exist. All they do is spread anger and try to rile people up and get people to be selfish like they are. I hate it. And then I wish horrible, horrible things on people like him, and then I realize that just by thinking that I'm horrible too and no better than they are."

"You could never be horrible. Wanting to stop someone from hurting others isn't horrible," Dillon said as he wrapped his arm around me and drew me against his side. "And we will stop him. You'll see."

Chapter Seventeen

ASH

By the time night fell, a strange calm had settled over me and the others on Team Van. Hayden's team had left to start their patrols thirty minutes ago and so far, no one had reported anything suspicious.

"I want you two here," Van told Dillon and me as he pointed at the check-in desk. The spot was centrally located, giving us a view of most of the public rooms in both the front and back of the building. "Keep an eye out and help as necessary."

We both nodded.

Dot, Van's deputy, frowned. "Why are they there?"

"Because that's where I want them," Van snapped. He immediately frowned, as if recognizing how short he'd been with her. "I want you mingling with the others, particularly the smaller shifters. As a deer shifter, you'll be a more calming presence than I will." Then he turned on his heel and left to talk to Doctor Roberts. The smile on

Van's face when he approached the doc made me do a double take. Was Van actually grinning?

That was… strange.

I'd been to see the local GP a couple of times since moving to Willow Lake. He was a quirky guy. I was never sure what to make of him. I mean, he looked like a university grad student who didn't have time for a haircut or a shave. But he was the doctor who all the supes in town went to. And, truthfully, he was nice and seemed to know his stuff, so I guess his appearance didn't matter.

"This was supposed to be my spot." Dot pouted.

"You're his deputy. I'm sure you have much more important things to do," I said, offering her a reassuring smile, even though I understood Van's reasoning. Dillon was a hellhound with more brute strength and cunning than any timid deer shifter, even one trained as a police officer. Hellhounds were designed by fate to be supernatural enforcers. If shit was going down, my money was on Dillon, not Dot, to stop it.

"I'm going to check upstairs again," Dot huffed and slunk away upstairs.

I don't know why she bothered—no one was supposed to be up there—but whatever. I leaned into Dillon's side and watched Van march from volunteer to volunteer, checking on them and bolstering the confidence of his makeshift militia like a seasoned general.

"I bet this situation would confuse the shit out of Parker and the other humans in town," I said to Dillon. "In all those human cop shows, the police always have to do things on their own. No one ever comes together to help them. It's so bizarre."

Dillon snorted. "Humans are bizarre, period."

I couldn't argue with that. As much as our shifter justice system had a lot of problems, I'd always believed the human one was just as flawed, if not more.

As sunlight faded from the sky, the tension in the room rose. A hush fell over us as everyone stared out the windows at the darkening landscape surrounding the inn. No one spoke. No one moved—well, except Simon Rivers, who I saw shift and crawl under a sofa. His shifted form was a housecat, and if the puffed-up state of his tail was anything to go by, he was petrified of what might happen. Poor guy. Not everyone had a big, growly hellhound at their side. The faint whir of the air conditioning was the only sound. I pulled the collar of my sweater closer to my neck as I fought off a shiver.

"Are you worried?" Dillon asked in a whisper.

I shook my head. "Not with you at my side."

Dillon squeezed my hand, then we went back to our silent vigil. Every few minutes Van's radio squawked with an update from Hayden. So far, no unwanted wolves had been spotted or scented on the lands around Willow Lake Inn, but something didn't feel right to me.

The back of my neck tingled, but I couldn't tell if it was from anticipation or warning. Dillon's eyes glowed with the fire of his beast.

"Something's…" I started but trailed off.

"Not right," Dillon finished. "I agree. What does your magic tell you?"

My first impulse was to brush off the idea my magic could tell me anything, but then I remembered this morning and how the power of it encircled Dillon and me, making him want to bite me. And then there was that tingling sensation earlier when I'd sensed the shifter magic. And I knew. Dillon was right. My magic still lived inside me. I just needed to remember how to use it.

I sucked in a deep breath and let it out slowly. Long ago lessons I'd learned as a young mage in a supportive coven filtered through my mind.

Step one: Concentrate on the place within me where my magic lives.

Once upon a time this first step had been as easy as breathing. My pulse raced. That weird but familiar pressure built inside me, and I prayed I wouldn't burp or fart. Dillon squeezed my hand. Right. I could do this. He'd seen the magic in me, right? And he never lied. I pushed aside my doubts and worries and shame as I hunted for the kernel of magical power that was mine and mine alone. My chest warmed slowly.

Step two: Push into that magic and embrace it.

The scars on my chest screamed in protest. Those thick cords of ruined flesh felt alive, twisting and writhing, as if they fought to contain and cage my magic. Sweat beaded across my forehead. Pushing past the pain, I forced myself to continue, fearing that a sneeze or burp or who knew what would come along and shatter my fragile progress.

The heat in my chest heaved and churned like lava in an active volcano, but I held tight to that little spark of energy until it grew and expanded and blossomed into something more—something nearly forgotten but so wonderfully familiar. Then my magic erupted, bursting free. It danced over my skin and through my veins. I exhaled softly at the joy of it. I lifted my hand and watched as fiery streaks of light bounced from one finger to the next.

"You are so beautiful," Dillon whispered reverently.

"It's really there." I smiled, wider than I had in years.

My eyes burned as I rubbed my chest, not because of my scars this time, but because it was where my magical core still lived. Magic thrummed through me, pulsing and dancing in rhythm with my heart.

"I don't think it ever left," Dillon said.

I toyed with my magic, letting the sensation of it ripple through me like laughter. I wanted to play. I wanted to rejoice. I wanted to show everyone I wasn't broken. Not anymore.

But we had work to do first.

I flung my magic outward and commanded it to hunt for intruders. Every elemental mage had the ability to do this. An air mage like my mother could sense the disruption of the air as people moved through it or simply stirred the air with their breaths. My brother, an earth mage, could feel the vibrations of footsteps over the land and the thrum of someone's heart beating in their chest. A water mage could sense the flow of blood rushing through someone's body, or so I'd been told—I'd never known a water mage well enough to ask them. For me, a fire mage, I could feel that spark of life that lived within each living being.

I cast my magic out, letting it slip over the inn's polished wood floors and through the miniscule gaps around the windows and doors until it rolled out over the landscape. There had been a time when even walls couldn't contain me, but my skills were considerably weaker than they had been. No, I shook my head. Dillon said I wasn't weaker; I was just out of practice.

Someone's phone rang.

I ignored it as I listened to my magic describe everything it encountered as it stretched out further and further. The tiny sparks of life from all the small woodland creatures in the forest around the inn pulsed along my magic. It was heady and beautiful, and I wanted to let my magic roll out and touch everything in the world.

Then Dillon was grabbing me, yanking me behind his back. My magic snapped back to me. I blinked and became aware of my surroundings again. Van was cursing, running toward us.

"What in the name of fire and flame are you doing?" Dillon demanded of the other hellhound.

"The basement," Van said as he dodged around us and grabbed for the door behind the counter and threw it open. "Sally says Jake had another vision and it had something to do with the basement."

I gathered my magic close, reveling at the feel of such power under my control, then I tossed it through the door and let it tumble down the steps.

"Intruders," I shouted. "There are intruders in the basement."

"Stay at your stations but get ready," Van shouted at the others as he rushed through the door with Dillon following at his heels.

Startled squeaks and chattering filled the air, but I didn't spare the rest of Team Van any other thought. Dillon was going to confront whoever was in the basement, and that was more important than anything else. Dillon might think he was my protector, but I refused to let anything happen to him either. I wouldn't let him face this without me.

The flickering light of flames licked at the darkened stairwell as the hellhounds transformed into their beasts and leapt into the shadows. The light of my magic jumped across my fingertips as I raced down after Dillon and Van. My magic was alive in me now and I couldn't remember the last time I'd felt so strong. I could do so much more than mere sparks now.

At first, I feared my magic had lied to me about there being intruders, because the dark basement was eerily silent. But as I cleared the last few steps and flew into the windowless subterranean room, I caught glimpses of several wolves brawling with the hellhounds. The scene had a ghoulish macabre atmosphere as dark wolves undulated through the uneven and ever-changing shadows created by the preternatural fire from the hellhounds' bodies.

And everything was absolutely silent.

This wasn't natural. Not at all.

The wolves who'd broken into my apartment had used an amulet with that kind of magic. These wolves had to be using the same thing.

I'd worked with magic my entire life up until Chris came along and tried to steal it from me. I had regularly merged my magic with members of both my family and my mother's coven, so even though it had been a long time, I could still tell how strange this was. Last night, during the attack at my apartment, I'd been torn awake, and in my disorientation and confusion I hadn't noticed the magic, not in any meaningful way.

But now that I was awake and alert, my magic was pulling in all kinds of details, like the fact that there were two sources of magic suppressing sound and smell. And that seemed even more bizarre. How were there two of these things?

Was my magic lying to me? Or was I so out of practice that I was misinterpreting what I felt?

I reached out with my magic again. I had to know what we were dealing with.

Two distinct and separate pulses of magic vibrated over me. The strongest one reminded me of a machine. It was devoid of the warmth and emotion that usually filtered through human-worked magic. In fact, the way my magic hummed through my bones in response to the mechanically driven energy made me suspect it was electrical. As a fire mage, that was one of my affinities.

Now that I'd figured that much out, I could sense the shape and pulse of it more clearly.

I'd bet anything that this magic was responsible for the unnatural suffocation of our senses. I didn't like it. At all. I couldn't imagine how disorienting it would be for a shifter to be in this situation. Their senses were usually heightened in their shifted form; to be without would be crippling.

At least the wolves were in the same predicament.

No howls rose in warning or in anger. No grunts exploded through the quiet as bodies collided. The bulky metal gate that appeared to protect the entrance of a roughly hewn tunnel on the far side of the room didn't clang when it was flung against the stone wall.

There was one thing I could do, though. I could give them a better look at their opponents. I didn't know where the light switch was—perhaps it was all the way back at the top of the steps—but I didn't need it. With a shaking hand, I swept my arm in a wide arc. The bare bulbs overhead flickered to life and filled the room with light.

I instantly regretted my actions.

It had been better not to see.

Bloodied and charred pieces of wolf shaped bodies littered the floor. Van and Dillon were ripping their teeth into even more wolves as the intruders struggled to crawl toward the tunnel opening in the far wall. I wanted to help but had no idea what to do. I'd never had to practice any offensive or even defensive magic. There were warrior covens out there, but mine hadn't been one of them.

But there had to be some other way I could help.

I scanned the basement, assessing the area for any other threats Van or Dillon might have missed in their mission to stop the wolves.

The room was filled with shelves. When this place was a pack house, the space had probably been used to store food, because large shifters like wolves had notoriously huge appetites. Most of the shelves were bare, so the neat stack of new looking cardboard boxes stood out. A few had been either tipped over or dropped during the skirmish, revealing a strange collection of... well, I didn't know what I was looking at. I didn't recognize any of it.

But even with a shaky hold on my newly reacquired magic, the magical aura of the items vibrated ominously

through the air. The back of my neck tingled uncomfort-
ably as I neared the artifacts. I was a few steps away when
my foot caught on a bright blue extension cord snaking
across the floor, leading to somewhere behind the boxes. It
was obviously out of place, so I followed it.

At first glance, the object at the end of the cord
appeared to be an old-fashioned gramophone. Although
the platform on the base was spinning around, no sound
emerged from the mouth of the brass-colored horn. That
had to be what was creating the unnatural suppression of
our senses.

Would it be better or worse to stop it?

What if I did the wrong thing?

My pulse thundered in my ears. I probably had enough
adrenaline pumping through me right now to fuel an army.
I needed to do something. I needed to help Dillon.

I had a history of doing the wrong thing, like trusting
Chris. And I hated that my ex was influencing me, even
now. But, at the moment, no one else knew for sure what
was happening here. That worked both ways. If the wolves
further in the tunnel heard the screams of their pack, would
they run away or come back to fight? Dillon and Van were
holding their own right now, but if they had to face a
whole pack…

Three wolves circled Dillon, nipping at the backs of his
hind legs and swiping at his face.

Shit. I was running out of time.

I was still staring at the machine when something hard
hit my back. Pain ricocheted through my side. What the
hell was that? Because it fucking hurt. I jolted upright and
spun around to find Dot brandishing a gun. It was so

strange to see the timid deputy waving a deadly weapon around that I couldn't make sense of it right away.

I couldn't hear her voice because of the machine, but it looked like she was shouting. At me? She didn't think I was helping the wolves, did she? But the way her surprisingly steady hands pointed the gun at the center of my chest, I decided maybe she did.

"Please, don't," I said, lifting my hands in surrender.

I started babbling more words. Words to distract her. Words to placate her. Words to beg her to be reasonable. I don't even know what exactly I was saying but it didn't matter anyway. They were silenced under the enchantment of the magical gramophone, just like everything else.

Her face contorted in another shout. I had no idea what she was saying, but this time she made a show of rubbing her finger along the trigger on her gun. *Shit, shit, shit.* She looked seconds away from pulling that damn trigger. I felt queasy and wobbly and lightheaded. I wasn't cut out to be face to face with the business end of a gun.

I needed to talk to her, have her hear what I was saying, make her realize I wasn't one of the bad guys.

That meant stopping the machine.

Decision made, I waved my hand toward the extension cord. Magic pulsed through me before shorting out the connection. It probably would have been cleaner to yank the cord from the wall, but I doubted Dot would tolerate me making any sudden moves.

Nothing changed.

Did my magic not work? I tore my gaze away from Dot's gun long enough to glance at the gramophone. It'd stopped spinning, which meant my magic had worked.

So why didn't I hear anything?

Fuck. It looked like I was right about there being two sources of magic.

The second had to be the amulet. I scanned the room. My eyes jumped from one charred body to the next. Nothing. Where the hell was it? I glanced at Dot, praying she'd give me a little more time. That's when I saw a strange bulge under her uniform. The longer I stared at the spot, the more my magic sang.

Well, fuck me, Dot was wearing the damn pendant.

That pressure in my chest I'd come to dread over the last several years filled me again. I opened my mouth to release the pressure with a burp. I was too slow. My ass vibrated in an all too familiar way.

Fuck. No. That wasn't supposed to happen. Heat burst over my face.

I looked around, an apology already falling from my lips. Except... no one could hear it.

Which meant no one could hear or smell the fart that'd just escaped either.

Thank Magic for that.

Damn it. I thought my magic was fixed.

The gun in Dot's hand jerked. I glanced up at her face. I really shouldn't have been staring at her chest because we both knew I hadn't been looking at her boobs. Not that that would have been better, but whatever. Dot narrowed her eyes at me.

Son of a drunken mage, she was going to shoot me.

I stared at the barrel of her gun. Was this really happening?

Her mouth twisted as her finger twitched. Then,

without conscious thought, magic shot out of my fingers and straight into the lump under Dot's uniform. The bright red glow of my fire magic engulfed whatever it was.

Dot's eyes widened. She wildly clutched at her shirt, her fingers tearing at the buttons. As soon as the first few buttons on her shirt popped open, I saw the pendant, exactly as Dillon had described.

The icy blue magic swirled in its dark depths in a mesmerizing pattern. Dot grabbed at the amulet and ripped it off. She flung it away. My magic followed the object's trajectory through the air. When the amulet hit the concrete floor, it broke in two. My magic seized its chance and dove into the fresh break, incinerating what was left of the suppressing magic.

The cacophony of clanging, screams, growls, crunching of breaking bones, and even sizzling flesh was deafening, but the smell was worse.

While shifters usually had stronger senses than other supes, a mage's senses weren't much different from a regular human's, or so I'd been told. Right now, I wished for even less than that. The air was laden with the sharp and overwhelming scent of blood and burned flesh. Nausea rolled over me, but I refused to succumb to it.

Dot jerked as the loudness of it all assaulted her. She was a deer shifter. I bet her flight response would burst into action in *one*, *two*…

And there it was.

She darted toward the stairs. But if she was wearing that amulet, there was only one place she would have gotten it. She was working with the damn wolves and there was no way I was letting her escape.

I dropped down to one knee and grabbed the extension cord. I yanked it, hard. My side pulled awkwardly, but I ignored the odd flash of pain as Dot tripped over the cord and fell forward. The gun flew from her hand and skidded across the floor. I dove for her before she could get any further. Even as I tackled her to the ground, I expected her to shift and gallop away. Instead, her whole body went lax in defeat.

With trembling hands, I fished the handcuffs off her belt and used them to secure her hands behind her back. I probably put them on too tightly, but I wasn't risking her getting away. As soon as she was taken care of, I flopped off her and scanned the room for other threats, but it looked like everything was finally under control.

None of the wolves were standing or even conscious. They weren't moving, so maybe they weren't even alive. Dillon and Van were going from person to person, sniffing at them. I gagged at the thought of purposely filling my nose with the stench of burned flesh.

Van's wish that no one be killed had obviously been overly optimistic.

An unexpected coldness swept over me as I eyed the carnage. I shivered. I was used to being cold but not like this.

But Dillon was alive and so was Van; that was all that mattered. Dot wiggled into a sitting position on the cold concrete floor, and I did the same. My arms were shaking something fierce, and my side was really starting to hurt now. Damn it. It looked like I was in shock or whatever. I'd be okay, though. I just needed a cookie, some juice, and a snuggle with my sexy hellhound under a warm blanket.

Van swung around to face us. His hellhound form faded away in a flash, but the fire of his beast danced in his eyes as he glowered at his deputy. He spit out a gob of blood and flesh, then wiped the back of his hand over his mouth. Bile shot up the back of my throat at the sight and I barely kept my supper down.

Dillon didn't change back to his human form. Instead, he edged closer to Dot, growling menacingly. Blood-soaked saliva dripped from his long sharp teeth as he pushed his face right up to hers. Dot quaked. Dillon didn't scare me, not even a little bit, but I could see where someone—particularly if they were on the wrong end of his anger—might find my boo scary as fuck.

The idea of it made me snort. I barely kept my wildly inappropriate laughter to myself. Why was I so giddy and lightheaded? It had to be the shock, right?

But now that I was thinking about it, I figured hell-hounds had probably inspired more than a few nightmarish horror movies. Silly humans, couldn't they see how pretty they were?

Especially Dillon. So pretty.

Wispy flames undulated along his fur, his fangs, and his claws. And the heat. So good. It poured off him. I shivered again. I hugged my arms over my chest and tried to warm myself. Stupid shock. Traumatic events sucked. I'd had more than enough of them in my life. It was time for them to stop.

Dillon stepped back from Dot to allow Van to approach his deputy.

"What the fuck were you thinking?" Van demanded. Smoke curled from his mouth.

Dot cowered.

"Dot," he barked. "Answer me."

"My sister. They have my sister." Tears streamed down her face. "They only wanted things. What were things compared to my sister? She's ten. A little kid. She doesn't deserve this."

"Fuck," Van muttered.

Static blasted out from the radio on Van's belt, which had somehow survived his transformation. Could all shifters do that? As much as I understood magic, shifter magic was in a league of its own.

Whatever the other person was trying to say, the message wasn't coming through. Let's face it, the basement probably wasn't the best place to get good reception. Van grabbed Dot and roughly hauled her to her feet, dragging her behind him as he went up the steps.

"Guard the fucking tunnel that no one fucking told me about," Van shouted over his shoulder. "I'll be right back. I need to tell Hayden to look for the girl."

Dillon, still in his hellhound form, stepped closer to me and whimpered. "Are you okay, little witch?"

"'M fine…" I slurred. I pushed myself onto my knees and peered at Dillon, trying to assess his body for injuries. "Are you hurt?"

"Ash… Something doesn't smell right. Are you…?" Dillon edged a little closer and lifted his head to sniff me. Remembering Dillon's warning about how badly I'd be burned if I touched his flames, I resisted the urge to reach for him, even if that's all I wanted to do. I wanted to curl up with my big, beautiful hellhound and sleep for the next seventy-two hours. At least.

So sleepy.

My eyes kept closing.

Damn it.

We had to find that girl. Then we needed to get our party started. We'd stopped the wolves. And I had a round of drinks to buy to celebrate getting my magic back. So many plans. Plans that did not involve sleeping. Sleep needed to wait. At least until after I'd had my way with my hellhound again. I moved to get up.

Except instead of standing, I fell. Forward. Face first. Right into Dillon's fiery hellhound body.

And then there was nothing.

Chapter Eighteen

DILLON

"Ash!"

No. This couldn't be happening.

Ash'd collided with my hellhound form. Fuck, fuck, fuck. My heart stopped for a moment, then pounded faster than ever. My shout came out as a howl for help as my shift erupted over me. As soon as my hands formed, I grabbed for the little mage. I didn't want to look, but I had to.

I rubbed my hands over my little witch's face and chest and arms and... He... He wasn't burned. I didn't know what had happened, but I wasn't sure if my heart would ever recover. He was okay. I exhaled harshly and gathered him close.

Then my hand hit something wet and warm.

The stench of blood was everywhere. But this... This was Ash's blood. Fuck. I'd sensed something was wrong with Ash, but why hadn't he said anything? I stood with Ash in my arms and bolted for the stairs.

"Help," I shouted. "Ash is bleeding."

And then Van was there, calling for an ambulance and showing me how to apply pressure over the hole—the fucking hole from a fucking bullet—in Ash's back. The local doctor, Roberts I thought his name was, came running over with an old-fashioned medical bag.

"I didn't mean to," Dot cried. "I'm sorry. I'm so sorry. I didn't think it was that bad. He… He seemed fine. I…"

She was lying. Smoke curled from my nostrils, and I snapped my teeth at her. The only thing keeping me from lunging for her was my need to care for Ash.

She cowered.

"Keep applying pressure," the doctor demanded, pulling my attention back.

She started muttering insincere apologies again, but her words were lost under my low incessant growling. Finally, someone hauled her away, so I didn't have to listen to her bullshit. If the doctor hadn't needed me to help him with Ash, I would have shut her the fuck up permanently, even if I doubted Ash would want me to kill her. He was too kindhearted and sweet and…

He was bleeding all over the damn floor.

If Ash died…

No. I couldn't think like that.

"He touched me," I said as I stared down at Ash. "He touched my hellhound, and he wasn't hurt."

Van sucked in a breath, then grabbed my shoulder and squeezed. "We'll save him, I promise."

"I don't understand. How could he…?" I looked up to meet Van's gaze.

"He's your mate," Van said. "Only a fated mate wouldn't be harmed by your hellhound."

"My mate." My breath hitched. I'd suspected as much, almost from the moment I'd seen him, but having it confirmed like this was bittersweet. Tears streamed down my face.

"Did you hear that, firecracker?" My voice broke as I whispered to Ash. "You're my mate. Which means you're stuck with me. So, you have to fight to stay here with me, you hear me? Always. It's going to be you and me. I knew you were special the moment I saw you on that road. I didn't know you would be my home, but I knew… Shit, Ash, you've got to stay with me."

Chapter Nineteen

ASH

What the fuck had happened?

I tried opening my eyes.

No dice.

I tried stretching. Holy fuck that hurt. My body ached everywhere, but especially my back. Then I became aware of more things: the muffled conversations, the annoying beeping, the squeak of someone's shoes moving over linoleum floors…

No. Not a hospital. Not again. After Chris, I'd had enough of hospitals to last a lifetime. I had to get out of here.

When I forced my eyes open, bright lights blinded me. My body jerked as I tried to sit up. Pain ripped through me.

"Fuck…" I moaned. Or maybe it was more of a sob.

"Stay there, little witch," a deep, but gentle voice

soothed as a large hand carefully guided me back to the mattress. "Calm down."

Some of my tension eased as I focused on Dillon, who was leaning over my bed. Dillon looked like shit, but then again, I doubted I looked much better considering I was the one hooked up to monitors and an IV.

"You're safe." Dillon held my gaze.

"Okay." I nodded. "Why am I here? What happened? I don't remember…"

"You were shot. In the back. Dot…" Dillon took a shuddering breath. "You didn't seem to feel it. So I guess that's good, right?"

"I feel it now," I whined.

"Yeah. The doctor said you were lucky. They had to sew you up inside and out, but they said the bullet going right through you was the best thing that could have happened." Dillon grimaced. "I'm sorry, Ash. By the time you got rid of that magic, Van and I were almost done. I should have known what was happening. I should have been there to help you. To stop her. I… Fuck…"

I swallowed. "It isn't your fault, Dillon. I remember enough of what happened to know that much."

"Fuck, Ash, you scared me." Dillon held my hand in his as tears flowed down his cheeks. "I just found you and you went and got yourself shot."

"Hey. But you didn't lose me, right? And I'm going to be okay." I wanted to brush the tears off my hellhound's face but twisting my body around so I could reach him didn't sound like the best plan. Instead, I pulled Dillon's hand close and kissed it.

"Your mom and brother are here. They stepped out to

grab a coffee a minute ago," Dillon said after he cleared his throat and blinked away the sheen in his eyes. "They should be back soon."

Which meant the only important person missing was Jeremy. I was surprised he wasn't here. I'd been in a bad place after my ex's attack and Jeremy had stayed with me for a long time. Dillon was my future, but Jeremy was my best friend, and he always would be. I had no idea how everyone kept magic hidden from him during my recovery, but he'd refused to leave my side. So I didn't think he'd abandon me now. I looked around the room, and sure enough there was a large candy arrangement. That had to be from him.

"That's from your friend Jeremy," Dillon confirmed, as if reading my mind. "He couldn't stay, but he was here for a few hours before your mother convinced him there wasn't anything he could do here. He looked ready to fight her, but there's a vampire on staff here. They worked some kind of mojo on him to make him change his mind."

I winced. I hated that someone messed with my best friend, but I understood. Even injured as I was, I sensed magic all around me, which meant the doctors were super-natural healers.

Mom must have told one of the nurses that we were determined to keep magic hidden from Jeremy. Guilt stabbed through me like another fucking bullet. The only reason he didn't know was because I had shied away from telling him. I could have—or more accurately—*should* have told him years ago. My mom had said I could after we turned sixteen. But after being best friends since elementary school, I wasn't sure how to confess my secret to him.

He'd be wildly excited to learn about supes, but what if he didn't forgive me for lying to him our whole lives? I was so damn selfish, but he was my best friend. I never wanted to lose him. Ever since I'd met Dillon, I'd been looking forward to them meeting for the first time. But… I guess maybe they already had. I was disappointed to have missed that.

"What's this about my son finding his mate and not telling his beloved mother?" my mother asked from the doorway.

She wore a teasing smile, but I could tell it was forced. Her arms were crossed as she tapped her tiny foot with an air of impatience. My mother had become the queen of hiding her feelings and distracting me after my last stint in the hospital. I could tell she was doing it again. Her usually bright eyes were dull. The lines on her face seemed to cut deeper. Her hair was standing up all around her head at odd angles. Her air magic was obviously zinging through her right now—probably ready to pounce on any possible threat.

My brother Birch was right behind her. He was slightly taller than my mom, so he peered at me over her shoulder. His pale face was even paler than normal, which was saying something. Yep, once again, everyone had come rushing to my hospital bed.

"Don't pester him too much, Mother, he just woke up," Birch said. He stared at me for a long moment. "You going to be okay?"

"Yeah. I think so." I nodded. "I'm sorry you both had

to drop everything to be here." I left off the *again*. *Like last time.* They knew. They didn't need me to say it.

"I'll go find a doctor or a nurse or something," Birch said. Then he lumbered out of the room. It wasn't that he was that big or anything, but he was stockier than either my mom or me and always seemed to move like a much, much larger man. Maybe it was because he was an earth mage.

As soon as he was gone, I thought back to what my mother had said when she'd first come into the room. I blinked at her. She was smirking now, and this time it didn't look as forced.

"Mate?" I asked. My gaze darted to Dillon, whose cheeks darkened.

"I didn't mean to tell your family before you. It just kind of came out."

"Back up, big guy," I said.

"I didn't know what it meant right away, because my parents were both hellhounds. Van explained it to me. When you fainted—"

"I did not faint." I scowled.

Dillon's lips twitched. "When you swooned—"

"Oh, fuck off."

"Such language," Dillon teased. "And in front of your mother too."

My mother snorted. Obviously, I hadn't been out of it long enough for Dillon to get to know Nerine Avery too well or he would know she had a potty mouth to rival a drunk undergrad at a frat party. She'd been on her best behavior when they'd talked on the phone. I doubt that would have lasted too long once she found out I was in the hospital again.

"Seriously though, you touched my hellhound form and weren't burned. Apparently mates can do that." Dillon tightened his hold on my hand. "Damn near gave me a heart attack."

"Mates." I smiled. "I like the sound of that."

Dillon grinned back at me. "Thank Magic for that. I'm not sure what we'd do if you didn't."

"You're stuck with me."

"Ditto," Dillon said.

"But… don't hellhounds live really, really long lives?" My chest tightened at the thought of him outliving me. If I really was his fated mate, he wouldn't have another chance at bonding with someone after I was gone. He'd live a long, lonely life. I didn't want that for him.

"We'll figure it out," Dillon said with another squeeze of his hand. And I wondered what he meant by that.

"Makes sense that my little fire bug would end up with a hellhound." My mother grinned. "Ashton never could resist fire."

The last thing I needed Dillon to hear were stories about my mishaps with fire. She was never going to let me forget about the trouble I had controlling my magic when I hit puberty. It didn't matter that none of what I'd done had been intentional—well, that wasn't entirely true. I'd known what I was doing when I set Mr. Ewing's car on fire.

Still, on Day one of our mating, Dillon didn't need to know the local human police had investigated me as a serial arsonist. Luckily another fire mage from my mother's coven had stepped in to teach me how to control my magic before things had gotten completely out of hand.

Before my mother could start her favorite stories about me, Birch came in with half a dozen people in his wake. I definitely owed him one for that. One person rushed forward to check my drugs, probably concerned with the dopey smile I had on my face as I stared at Dillon. I doubted I needed to be looked at by so many doctors and nurses, but I knew Birch's way of coping was to demand everyone in the damn hospital come and see to me.

Doctor Roberts was at the head of the group. As a sphinx shifter, he was well aware of the Eternal Magic and how it helped to heal. It was strange to see him look as unkempt as usual in this setting, but I relaxed at the sight of him. His light brown hair was longer now than the last time I'd seen him, curling around his head in a big, tangled mess. And the whiskers on his jaw were somewhere between scruff and a beard, just like always.

"Hello, Ash," the doctor said with a smile as he approached. "How are you feeling? You look a lot better than the last time I saw you."

"Good," I said, and I meant it as I glanced at Dillon again. He'd let go of my hand and sat back to give the medical staff room to work. I was just glad they hadn't asked him or my family to leave, although I doubted they would have left even if they were asked to.

After they checked me over, the doctor smiled. "I'm sure you already know this, but your connection to your magic has also improved since your last physical."

My eyes locked on the doctor's. "Do you know why?"

"I suspect it is because you met your mate. The trauma

your body suffered previously interrupted your connection to your magic. The magic was still there, you just weren't able to access it. When you met your mate, your magic was drawn to his and found new ways to surface. Your magic isn't fully recovered yet, but with time I expect you will gain full use of it again."

I reached for Dillon and grabbed his hand. It was lucky I was seated because I think my legs would have given out. I knew something had changed, obviously, because I'd recently used my magic for the first time in years, but having the doctor confirm what I'd suspected made relief bloom in my chest. It was real.

"Oh, baby, that's wonderful," my mom squealed.

And, as much as I hated waking up in a hospital again, I suddenly knew everything was going to be okay. Better than okay, even.

Chapter Twenty

ASH

I tilted my phone so Dillon, who was currently in his hellhound form and dripping in preternatural flames, wouldn't be in the picture as I answered Jeremy's video call. My mom and brother had finally left the apartment to pick up some groceries. It was the first time they'd left my side since I'd been released from the hospital, and I'd seized the opportunity to cuddle with my hellhound on the couch.

"I can't believe they already let you out of the hospital," Jeremy said before I could even say hello. He leaned back in his chair and crossed his arms. He was jiggling a little, so I imagined he was tapping his foot too. "I knew I shouldn't have left. What kind of country bumpkin doctor releases someone with a gunshot wound after only two nights in the hospital? You were still unconscious yesterday morning for pity's sake. Did they do any tests? Did they send you home with instructions? Was that doctor even awake when he examined you? Because he looked like he'd just rolled out of bed."

Dillon lifted his head, turning his snout toward me. If he'd been in his human form, he probably would have lifted an eyebrow. I patted him on his toasty warm head to let him know he didn't have to worry. The flames on his black furry coat curled around my fingers. Man, I loved that I could touch him like this.

"I'm fine, Jer, I promise." And I was. I wasn't healing as fast as most supes, but considering how disconnected I'd been from the Eternal Magic for the last seven years I was doing pretty good—good enough that the doc had sent me home.

"Pfft. You have a hole in your back, Ash. You're not fine."

"The doc sewed me up, and then there wasn't much more they could do for me. The bullet didn't hit anything important like my heart or my lungs or whatever."

Jeremy frowned. "You are important. The bullet hit you."

Dillon grunted, like he agreed with Jeremy.

"I love you too, Jer. But, seriously, you don't have to worry about me."

He leaned toward his camera. His blue eyes stared straight into mine. "You are my best friend. Of course, I'm going to worry."

I loved Jeremy with all my heart. I wished I hadn't been such a coward when we were teens, and then maybe I wouldn't have to keep so many secrets from him. Jeremy, I was sure, didn't hide a single thing from me. He was the most open and honest person I'd ever met. He said once that it was because he was the youngest of seven kids. With a family that big, all living together in a little midcentury bungalow, keeping secrets had been impossible, so he'd just stopped trying to do it.

It was one of the other reasons I'd never told him about supernatural beings. It wasn't natural for him to keep secrets. He'd be a mess if he tried to keep such a big one from his family.

"Tell me about your new job."

Jeremy rolled his eyes. "Not a very subtle way to change the subject."

I smirked. "Was I supposed to be subtle?"

"Fine, Mr. Black Knight." He huffed, but his blue eyes twinkled. "I'll tell you about my new job, but only because you look and sound better than I'd thought you would. I'll pretend it was just a scratch if that's what you want."

"A mere flesh wound," I agreed with a grin.

Dillon tilted his big hellhound head in obvious confusion. Had he not seen *Monty Python and the Holy Grail?* We'd have to fix that. I scratched him behind the ear, and he dropped his head to my lap again. I sighed as the heat from his fiery body sank into me. He was so much better than any blanket.

"My boss is a little… odd, but the pay is good."

"And you just go to farmers' markets with her? That's it?"

He nodded. "I might not even need to pay for highlights in my hair this year. I'm getting a lot of time in the sun."

"Do you sell lots?"

"Not a single thing so far." He snorted. "But she

doesn't seem to care, so whatever. I get to read a lot. Right now, I'm getting my fix of sexy gay vampires. You should definitely read the series so we can gush about the hot as fuck hero." He sighed like he couldn't imagine anything sexier than a vampire. Of course, he probably wouldn't do that if he knew his childhood neighbor was a vampire. That man was an uptight bitch. A true male Karen before being a Karen was a thing. Then again, now that I was an adult, I could sort of see that living next door to a house with seven very active and loud boys might be challenging.

"What about your writing?"

Jeremy glanced away. "I'm working on some ideas."

He was always working on ideas. I didn't know if he'd ever finish a book, but I wanted that for him.

Then his eyes lit up. "Actually, you should tell me all about that boyfriend of yours."

"What do you want to know?"

"So…" He pulled a crumpled looking coiled notebook from his backpack and started flipping through the pages. "I may have written down some questions." He flashed me a page full of scribbles.

"You have that many questions? About Dillon?"

He waggled his eyebrows. "You know me. I'm always looking for inspiration. Maybe you and Dillon could be the heroes of my next novel. You know, I was thinking maybe I should write something paranormal. This vampire series is smokin' hot. I bet I could write something like that, but with something other than vampires so it isn't exactly the same. Oh… Dillon could be a bear shifter. And…" He stroked his chin. "You could be a little twink-ish fox shifter. Or maybe a cat? Something cute like an ocelot. I haven't decided yet."

Dillon had started growling softly at the idea of him being cast in Jeremy's non-existent novel as a bear shifter.

"Uh…"

"Would it be easier if I texted my questions to you?"

I swallowed. How many things would I have to lie about? When I didn't answer immediately, he pointed his finger at me.

"Don't get all prudish now. I want all the deets. Where did you meet? Was it love at first sight? Were his parents both giants too? Where is he from? Does he have any brothers? A series about some brothers would be fun, don't you think? Hmm… Do you think if he is a bear shifter his brothers would be too? Or maybe a shifter's animal isn't a genetic thing. What do you think? Does he like the woods? Is he proportional, if you know what I mean…?" He leered at me.

"Text them," I blurted, knowing full well where Jeremy's questions were going from there.

He nodded sharply. "Will do."

A yawn broke free before I could stop it.

"Shit," he said. "You're probably worn out. I shouldn't have talked so much. You make sure your big bear of a boyfriend takes you to bed. But don't let him do anything more than that."

"Yes, Doctor Jeremy," I said.

As soon as the call ended, a text popped up on my phone. Oh boy. His questions went on and on. How the hell had he typed them all in so fast?

"He seems nice," Dillon said. "I didn't get a chance to talk to him much when he came by the hospital."

I nodded, still scrolling through the questions. Another yawn hit me as I said, "He's my best friend."

I expected him to ask why Jer didn't know about supes if he was my best friend, but he didn't. Instead, he jumped off the sofa and shifted into his human form.

"Come on," he said with his hand extended to me. "Let's go cuddle in your bed for a while."

I wished cuddling was a euphemism, although falling asleep in Dillon's arms was pretty awesome too.

Chapter Twenty-One

ASH

"Are you sure you're ready for that?" Dillon asked as he mouthed hot kisses along the side of my neck. I knew he was trying to distract me, and I thoroughly loved his approach. I wasn't going to let him win, but I twisted my head to give him more access to my neck anyway.

I was straddling his lap and took the opportunity to grind against him. A pang of discomfort zinged through my back at the movement, but I wasn't going to stop now. My mother and brother had gone home a few days ago, and Dillon and I had been all over one another since the door shut behind them. Most of the time, Dillon insisted on sticking to blow jobs and nothing more. I understood why he was still being cautious, and I wasn't about to complain about getting regular blow jobs, but that didn't stop me from wanting more.

Even before releasing me from the hospital two weeks ago, Doctor Roberts had told us we could have sex as long as we were gentle and careful. Dillon hadn't trusted that news until I'd dragged the doctor back in and had him explain everything to my hellhound all over again. Dillon's face had turned every shade of red imaginable, but he'd still asked more questions than I had.

During that talk, I'd finally come to understand why he was so worried about me. Apparently, shifters healed more quickly than mages, and often didn't have scars to show at the end, the lucky bastards. My healing was even slower than a typical mage because my magic had still been recovering when the attack had happened. So the fact that I wasn't healing as quickly as he would have and had another scar on my body had freaked him out and made him conclude I was in worse shape than I really was. In the end, though, I think we'd both been happy with what the doctor said, or so I'd thought at the time.

Or maybe Dillon's interpretation of gentle and careful was different from mine.

Again. To be clear. I wasn't complaining. Any chance to have Dillon close was good, but I was looking forward to when being gentle and careful were no longer necessary, and where having a mouth on my cock was foreplay to more strenuous activities, not the end game.

I wanted that wild hellhound who was so overwhelmed by my awesomeness that he bit me when he climaxed. Gentle and cautious Dillon was awesome too though; I couldn't remember ever having such amazing sex with someone before. Not that I'd had tons of experience, but still. He was better than them all, especially Chris. Being with Dillon was mind-blowing. Every. Single. Time.

"Yes, I'm sure." I hissed as his fingers pinched my

nipples. I'd never been much for nipple play, but Dillon made even that sexy.

His hands brushed down my body before sliding around to cup my ass. I knew he was into this as much as I was since his hands were wickedly hot. I'd started noticing all kinds of little details in the last few weeks, like how his hellhound form was always close to the surface when we were like this. And now that we knew I couldn't be hurt by his magic, I'd been thinking about how his flames might feel against my body when I fell asleep at night. I bet they'd keep me warm all night long.

"We could stay in and do this all night," he murmured against my ear.

And it was tempting. Truly.

But I knew my hellhound well enough to know that pretty soon he'd start worrying that we were doing too much and that my body couldn't handle that much sex.

And I refused to binge watch another series tonight. I just couldn't do it. Even with him at my side, I was going stir crazy.

I needed to get out.

"We can do more of this when we get back." I was panting, but based on his defeated groan, I knew he'd heard me.

"Fine," he grunted and loosened his grip on my ass.

"Hey, what are you doing?" I pulled back and scowled at him.

"I thought you wanted to go to the pub."

"I do, but you can't get me all worked up and leave me like this. There's lots of time to take care of each other here first before we head over there."

Dillon grinned at me as his arms snaked around me again.

"Priorities, big guy," I said as I rolled my hips against him. "And you are always my first priority."

Within minutes, our clothes were off. Then I was staring into Dillon's eyes with the knowledge I was the luckiest guy in all of Willow Lake, maybe the world. Dillon's gaze strayed down to my chest, but I didn't feel anxious about my scars anymore. At least not with him. Besides, I now had a couple more, and I couldn't be precious about them all, right?

Maybe next summer I'd even go shirtless down at the beach along Willow Lake.

Or not.

Hellhounds didn't like the water. And I wasn't going anywhere without my hellhound.

"Let's move to the bedroom," Dillon said.

Yeah. Probably a good idea. As much as I wanted to ride my hellhound hard, I wasn't sure my body could handle that yet. We could find more comfortable positions on the bed. I slid off his lap and held out my hand for him. Hand in hand, we walked to the bedroom. I swayed my ass since I was in front of him. It was better to distract him with my perky ass rather than have him fixate on my newest scar.

I didn't want him to back out now.

Once in bed, I turned so my ass was facing him. I figured bottoming wouldn't hurt my side as much. Man, I was looking forward to having everything fully healed. I couldn't wait to get my big hellhound under me again.

Dillon grabbed my monster bottle of lube. When I'd

purchased it, I thought it'd probably last me a year or more. The bottle was shockingly low now. We'd have to start buying it by the case load. I snorted at the idea.

"What? What's the matter?" Dillon stopped what he was doing to look at my face. His lube covered hand was inches away from my ass.

"Nothing." I wiggled my ass. "Come on, I'm ready. I want you in me this time."

He wasn't going to distract me again this time with blowjobs or frotting, damn it.

His hands were hot when he touched me. I groaned when he traced my hole before pushing the tip of one thick finger inside. The lube was warm and slippery against my skin. I pushed against him, and his finger slipped in deeper.

"So freaking good," I muttered as his finger slid in and out. I moaned and groaned and urged him to go faster, but Dillon ignored me. He would never do anything that might hurt me, especially in bed.

Finally, he kissed me before guiding me to my side. He came up behind me and wrapped his arms around me. The solid heat of his body against mine from head to foot was addicting. In this position, I would miss seeing his face when he came, but I loved being wrapped in his arms.

My mother had asked how I could stand being so close to Dillon all the time when his body temperature ran so high, but I was becoming addicted to his heat. I'd told her it was because I was a fire mage, but it was more than that. I'd been so cold for so long, I didn't think I'd ever get to the point where I felt too warm.

And... fuck... why was I thinking about my mother when Dillon was about to stick his dick up my ass?

All thoughts scattered when the blunt crown of his cock pushed against my hole. My breath caught and I savored the feel of his body entering mine. His heated breath fanned across my shoulders. I grabbed one of his hands in mine and held it tight, loving how I could feel him everywhere. Inside and out.

When he finally sank all the way in, his arm wrapped tightly around my stomach and held me close. We stayed that way for several long heartbeats.

"I love you, my little witch," Dillon whispered.

"I love you too." I kissed his hand, wishing I could twist around enough to kiss his mouth, but my body couldn't do that yet.

"I didn't think I'd ever find you, but I did. You are my home. Before you, I was lost."

My eyes burned at his words, and I let a few tears fall. "You'll never be lost again, Dillon. You're mine forever."

"And you're mine too. My mate."

My breath hitched at his words.

Fuck the pain. I needed to see his face. I pulled away from him just long enough to flip around, then joined our bodies again. Whatever pain I'd expected to feel wasn't there, as if the Eternal Magic was protecting me in this moment, encouraging me to be with my mate so completely.

My mate. I grinned. I loved that word.

As if triggered by just that thought alone, the crimson glow of my magic erupted from me for the first time since I'd been shot. Dillon's golden orange magic rushed to meet it. Our individual magics pulsed with a joyful and excited rhythm until they blended so completely it was impossible to see where one started and the other ended.

As Dillon rolled his hips back before rocking gently into me again, our joined magics embraced us. Yes. This was how it was supposed to be. Me and him. Together so completely that we became one, as if the power of our united magic fused every part of our lives together.

Our joined magic took on a rhythm of its own, becoming wild and frenetic. The faster it thrummed around us, the more it pulled on the well where my magic lived deep inside me. This was the Eternal Magic. The part of it that lived within Dillon and me. I pushed into the sensation, feeling warmth and acceptance and beauty as I stared into my mate's fiery eyes.

Euphoria burst through me, and the way Dillon gripped me, I knew he felt it too.

"My mate," I whispered against his lips. Then he echoed the words before sealing our lips together in a heated kiss.

As soon as our mouths parted, a new sensation welled between us.

Then ancient and magical words surged up within me, overwhelming me until they broke free and slipped over my tongue. Words I swore I'd never heard before. Words I didn't understand. But I wasn't scared because my instincts told me this was the Eternal Magic, which was as familiar to me as life itself.

Dillon stared into my eyes as similar words fell from his lips.

Our joined magic became even more luminous and

vivid with each murmured word. Then in a radiant blast of light, it rippled over us. Awe filled me as my brain finally understood the gift we'd been given. We were more than just one another's chosen mates. Our souls had been bound together by the Eternal Magic herself. She'd offered a primal and potent blessing to us, and we'd accepted it. Nothing but death could divide us now.

As the ancient words faded, our bodies took on a frantic rhythm of their own, driving me to my climax. I cried out Dillon's name as I came. Dillon grunted, as if surprised when my body tightened around him. Then his mouth clamped onto my neck; teeth sinking into my flesh. Our joined magic flared around us in a throbbing incandescent orb, before exploding in a blast of fiery embers, which fell harmlessly to the bed around us. I trembled in my mate's arms as I tried valiantly to come all over again.

When my heart finally settled, my brain filled with questions.

"Dillon?" I was cuddled against his hot body, and it felt like I was basking in the sun.

"Yes, firecracker?"

I grinned. With the explosion of magic and light we'd just shared, my nickname fit perfectly.

"Was that what I think it was?"

"A mate bond?"

"Yes. My coven calls them soul bonds, but yeah. I mean, it seems like it might have been, but I didn't think those happened in real life. I thought it was all just a myth, to be honest."

Dillon brushed his hand over my back. "There was a couple at the inn the night of the attack who I thought might be bonded. They had matching streaks of turquoise in their hair."

"You mean Mercer and Oak? Wait…" I pushed myself up so I could look at my sexy hellhound. I blinked at him. "Holy Magic…"

"What?"

"You… You have a…" I brushed my fingers over the side of his neck. "You didn't have a tattoo here, did you? I mean, I don't remember one, but…"

"No, I didn't." Then his gaze dropped down to my own neck. His breath hitched. "Does it look like a flame?"

I swallowed and reached up to touch the spot he was staring at. The texture of my skin didn't feel any different, but heat emanated from that spot. "I have one too?"

He nodded. The red and orange flames on his neck undulated like actual fire as he swallowed. "Is that okay?"

I leaned closer to look at his marking. "Do that again."

"What? Why?"

"It moved."

His eyes dropped to mine again. "Yours is moving too, not a lot, but enough that it doesn't look like a regular tattoo."

I blinked. That was… Magic, I guess. "Are you okay with being bonded to me? I feel like we didn't talk about it. It's a pretty big thing, right? We probably should have talked about this. I mean, I'm okay with it, but what about you? And what does it mean? Do you know? Are the myths true do you think?"

Dillon smiled at me as he pulled me into his arms. "It's okay, firecracker. I'm thrilled to be joined with you. And it is an honor to receive a blessing like this from the Eternal Magic. I am humbled and so damn happy."

I relaxed in his arms. "Are you sure?"

"Yes. As for what it means? I think our lives are joined now. My parents were bonded like this. They said it was a rare gift from the Eternal Magic. Our energies are combined now so that our lifespans will match from this moment on. Unless one of us meets an unnatural death, we will never have to live without each other."

"Wait, how old are you? I feel like we should have had this conversation a while ago. Maybe I was too scared to ask. And, let's face it, we had a lot of shit going on. But it seems like something I should know."

Dillon pressed a kiss to my head and hugged me tighter. "I'm a little over three hundred."

My jaw dropped. "Seriously?"

"My parents weren't big on birthdays, so they never really tracked my age. But my appearance hasn't changed much since I hit about thirty. I don't know much about hellhounds and how they age. My parents left when I was thirteen and I haven't seen any other hellhounds until I met Van."

"They left you when you were thirteen? What the fuck?" I pushed up on to my elbow and looked at him, ignoring the ache in my side. I couldn't imagine being abandoned at that age.

"I'm not going to lie. It was hard in the beginning. And I don't really know what happened to them. One day they were there, then they weren't."

"They disappeared?"

"I searched for years for them. I've never found them.

Eventually I realized they weren't coming back, and I'd have to live my own life." He looked at me. "But I never stopped looking for a place to belong again. And I found it, with you."

"I love you so damn much," I said. "We're going to have the best fucking life together. I want to spend an eternity with you. Mages live a long time, but not as long as a lot of other supes. But with this bond, we can, can't we?"

"I think so." Dillon swallowed hard. "It's something we can ask around about. Your mom's coven might have more information about hellhounds or mixed mate bonds. If not, maybe Van or even that couple, Mercer and Oak, might know something."

"I hope we're right. I don't want to leave you alone." I hugged him so damn tight.

"But I don't want to think about dying right now," he said. "I want to enjoy every second of the time I have with you."

Chapter Twenty-Two

ASH

An hour or so later, I managed to drag Dillon out of the house. I was feeling fantastic. My magic had never felt stronger. Dillon was my mate. It was time to celebrate and shout it to the world. When we arrived at the parking lot at the Willow Lake Inn, Dillon's hand tightened over mine.

"Are you sure?" he asked. Again. For the millionth time. Like going to the place where I'd been shot would be traumatic for me.

Weirdly, though, I wasn't worried about that, which probably had a lot to do with how safe I felt with Dillon, even though he was always quick to point out he'd been right there with me when I'd been shot and hadn't been able to protect me.

Someday, I hoped to convince him he needn't feel guilty about that. None of it had been his fault.

We walked very slowly toward the ornately carved wooden doors of the Willow Lake Pub.

Okay, so maybe I wasn't fully ready for all the sex and all the walking and all my regular activities all at once, but I was getting there. I'd already called Parker about going back to work and was scheduled for half-days starting next weekend. Parker assured me I didn't have to rush my recovery and that my job would be waiting for me when I was ready, but I wanted to get back to normal. Dillon, my grumpy, over-protective hellhound, hadn't been impressed by my back-to-work plans.

Unfortunately, I wobbled a little as we crossed the last few steps to the door. Damn it. Now he was going to worry even more. His hand rested lightly on my back—carefully avoiding the spot where I'd been shot—and he stayed slightly behind me, as if ready to catch me if my legs suddenly decided to give out.

"If you're tired, we can leave." He was so predictable.

"The doctor said moving around and staying active would be good for me," I said as I waited for Dillon to open the heavy door.

"I don't think going to the pub was what he had in mind," he muttered.

Dillon was probably right, but we'd already come all this way. We might as well go in for a few minutes, right? Besides I was beyond ready to leave the apartment. I'd never spent so much time in my apartment, and I was going stir crazy, even with a sexy hellhound there to distract me.

It was funny how when my mother and my brother fussed over me, it irritated me no end and made me want to push harder to establish my independence, but when

Dillon did it, I usually wanted to cuddle close and assuage the big guy's worries. But even that could only work for so long. I needed to be out with people.

As soon as we entered the pub, Paws let out a surprisingly feline-sounding yowl in greeting and everyone turned toward us and started clapping. My cheeks heated. Okay. I hadn't expected that.

"Enough, enough," I said, waving my hand through the air.

We made our way to a small round table in the center of the pub and Dillon helped me ease into a seat. As soon as I was settled, Dillon left to get drinks for us. I doubted my darling hellhound would bring back anything interesting. Hell, I'd be lucky if he returned with a cola. But that was okay. I didn't need alcohol tonight. Paws jumped onto the table, obstructing my view of Dillon's ass as he leaned against the bar. The cat stared unblinkingly at me.

"You look like shit." The cat emphasized his point with a sharp flick of his tri-colored tail.

"Are you insulting me? Because the big fiery hound over there might take exception to that."

"Oh, please," Paws said. "As if I'd ever be scared of a hellhound."

Which again begged the question: what was Paws? Even with my magical powers almost fully recovered, I couldn't identify the cat's magical energy. Maybe I should ask Dillon and see if he knew.

Dillon returned a moment later with our drinks. I eyed the white liquid. Then I sniffed it.

"Milk? Really?"

Dillon lifted his own glass of the same and clinked it to mine. Paws stared at my glass, then leaned forward more and more until his nose was mere millimeters from the milk.

"Hey," I shouted at him and pulled my glass closer. "If you want milk, Dillon will get you your own."

Paws jerked back and started cleaning his fur with frantic little licks.

"Are you embarrassed?" I laughed.

Paws hissed at me and resumed his bath, right there in the middle of the table.

Dillon looked around the pub, pausing now and then to study the way the humans mingled with the supes. On the day of the attack, supes of every kind had come out to defend our town, but this wasn't the same. This was just an average day in Willow Lake.

I could see where it'd be a bit of a novelty to see such a wide range of different supernatural beings all socializing together and with humans too. Most humans wouldn't linger where supes hung out, complaining about the weird vibe. Honestly, for me, that magical energy was one of the many things that made Willow Lake so special. Maybe it was the same for some humans, maybe some were more comfortable with its effects than others.

I used to think humans were stupid for not recognizing the predators in their midst, but I wasn't so sure about that now. Even supes couldn't always sense the ones who'd prey on others. I could only hope that coming together and protecting one another would become the norm rather than the exception. That was the only way to build a stronger community, right?

At the moment, Dillon's attention was on Parker, my ginger-haired boss at the Flying Rowan Café, who was flirting with Levi, the owner of the town's motel. The poor minotaur was huffing and blushing as he rubbed the back of his neck and stammered out a response to something Parker had asked. The guy was terribly shy, but that didn't seem to bother Parker one bit. It wasn't that long ago I had considered the big, broad minotaur as possible dating material, but I hadn't entertained that thought for long. Parker had obviously already called dibs, even then.

"They'll figure it out. Eventually," Van said as he sat down at our table and saw who we were watching.

"Hey, Van. When we talked earlier, I thought you said you wouldn't be able to get here until later," Dillon said as he smiled at the other hellhound. Then his eyes darted to me.

I pretended not to notice. I knew they'd talked earlier, although I was sure Dillon thought I'd been sleeping. It was obvious from the side of the conversation I'd heard that my hellhound had asked Van to look into my ex and his incarceration. Whatever Van had told him had appeased Dillon, which made me think Chris was not doing well. I couldn't decide how I felt about that.

Seeing Dillon and Van together now made me think they were well on their way to creating a mini hellhound pack of two. I also didn't think it'd be long before Van formally asked Dillon to start training as a deputy. They'd both been hinting at that since the attack and there was a rather obvious vacancy in the police department now.

"How did it go today?" I asked. The Supernatural Council had taken custody of Dot that afternoon.

Van took a long draw from his pint glass—at least someone got to have beer—and then set it down with a thump. "I don't know what they'll do with her honestly. It wasn't that many years ago that they would have let her go, because no one died from her actions. They would have let the disciplinary actions fall to the local alpha of her herd, but without an alpha in Willow Lake, the SC has to step in. They are still so new to all this, having to figure out on a case-by-case basis what kinds of punishments are suited for which kinds of crimes. Since she was my deputy, holding a position of trust in the community, I expect her punishment might be harsher. But who knows what they'll decide."

Yeah. I knew all about the SC's changes, for obvious reasons. The system wasn't perfect, but it was better than it had been before.

"Dot's being cooperative," Van continued. "She knows she fucked up, but she doesn't have a lot of answers. Her sister doesn't remember anything about her abduction either. But, at the same time, I know Dot's lying to me. Even now. I just don't know why or what she's lying about. The situation is irritating the shit out of me. Something's been going on with her for a while. I can only hope she hasn't been mixed up with the wolves all this time."

I had mixed feelings about Dot. On some level, I understood the impulse to save her sister, but she should have talked to Van. And she shouldn't have shot me in the back. Obviously.

"It's weird they dumped the kid right after phoning Dot, isn't it?" Dillon asked.

A local rancher had found the ten-year-old tied up but otherwise physically unharmed about a quarter mile from town the morning after the robbery. She'd been found on the opposite side of town from the inn, so nowhere close to where the shifters had been patrolling. The poor girl had been out there all night.

Van rolled his shoulders. "Robbie is saying the wolves we killed had been acting alone. Says they probably tossed the girl because they'd already got what they needed from her, by making Dot do what they wanted. The last time he was under investigation he used some of his wolves as scapegoats too."

Dillon frowned. "So Rob gets away with all this? My testimony didn't help?"

"It's your word against his."

"But he can't lie," I said, pointing at Dillon.

"You know that, and I know that, but the SC says that hasn't been proven conclusively."

"That's fucking bullshit," I muttered as I downed the rest of my milk and slammed my glass on the table. Honestly, it didn't have the same impact as downing a mug of beer or a shot of whiskey or even a glass of that fruity wine my mother liked.

Van stared at his glass grimly. "I'm thinking of calling in some outside help."

"From the SC? That's the only option, right?"

The hellhound grunted but didn't clarify what he meant.

"Do you think Dot did anything else?" I asked after a minute or two.

"We're going through her files and all that shit…" Van

grimaced. "We haven't found anything yet and I pray we don't."

Then the energy shifted.

I scanned the room. The last time something like that happened, Jake had a vision. This time it was just Hayden coming in. He'd thrown open the door to the pub and was stalking toward our table. His eyes were flashing, showing how close his wolf was to the surface. His hair was flying out in all directions, like he'd been pushing his fingers through it in agitation.

"What the hell are you doing here?" the wolf asked. The question sounded gruff, but there was affection in his tone.

He grabbed Dillon's shoulder and surreptitiously rubbed his wrist against the hellhound's neck, scenting him, marking him as one of his pack—even if Hayden refused to call it that. Then he did the same to me and Van before claiming one of the empty chairs at the table. He even reached over and scratched Paws behind the ear.

Paws ignored us all, despite having two more people join our table since he'd started giving himself a bath. I watched the cat twist around to lick the fur on his back, like the creature was providing a weird sort of entertainment.

Having rubbed his scent on to us, Hayden's shoulders relaxed a little. He might not openly acknowledge he was Willow Lake's alpha, but every little thing he did showed actions were stronger than words. Maybe Dillon was right about that.

"I went to your apartment, and you weren't there. You

just got out of the moon-cursed hospital; why aren't you at home?"

Dillon looked at me with an I-told-you-so expression.

"The pub has the best cow juice in town, didn't you know?" I lifted my empty glass with its milky residue. "I had to get my fix."

Hayden rolled his eyes and muttered something I couldn't quite catch. Van and Dillon both laughed, so obviously they'd heard. Whatever. I was still happy I'd forced Dillon to bring me here. To my way of thinking, routines and normal everyday life were always underrated. Before I'd met Dillon, going to the pub and being with the other Willow Lakers was part of my routine. I'd needed this to feel normal. I needed to believe we would all be fine.

Jake wandered over a few minutes later.

"Did you want a drink, Hayden?"

"You didn't have to come over, kid," Hayden said, turning his intense gaze on the bartender. "I was coming over to see you at the bar as soon as I'd growled at these two for a few minutes."

"It's no bother," Jake said, blushing under the alpha's attention. Then Jake's gaze darted to Van and Dillon.

The oracle's eyes lingered a little too long on Dillon to be entirely innocent in my opinion, but I couldn't fault the guy for looking. Dillon was a beautiful sight to behold. It looked like both Jake and I had a type, making it clear we never would have worked out, if we had ever tried dating.

"I wanted to thank all of you for stopping the break-in. I still don't understand what happened, what with the gas leak and then the robbery, but… At least nothing much was stolen." Jake worried his hands as his gaze bounced around the table before landing on me. "And, Ash, I feel awful about you getting shot trying to save a bunch of my grandfather's weird junk." He swallowed. "Your drinks are on the house from now on."

"Oh, that's not—"

"I insist." Jake wasn't normally a bold or assertive guy, but his tone said he wasn't going to change his mind about this.

"Thank you," I said, conceding to him. "Is much missing?"

"Honestly, I don't know. I don't think so, but..." Jake shrugged. "I suppose I should go through my grandfather's things at some point. I just... Well, it feels wrong somehow."

I wasn't sure if that was because most of the items were magical relics or because they had belonged to a grandfather he hadn't really known. Either way, it had to be weird for Jake. Especially since he didn't know about supernaturals. Yet.

Come to think of it, maybe Jake shouldn't go through anything by himself anyway. Who knew what he might toss or give away?

"If you want help," I said, putting my hand on Jake's arm. "You let me know, okay?"

"Yeah. Okay." Jake nodded, but he didn't sound convinced.

He wandered back to the bar after taking Hayden's order.

"The kid is wrong. It's like his inability to see supes is making him stupid," Paws said as he sat regally at the center of the group. His newly bathed calico coat was shiny and tidy.

"You finished the inventory yet?" Van asked.

"Wait. What inventory?"

Van stroked his chin. "Right. I guess you haven't heard. After the attack, we went hunting through the inn, trying to figure out where Dot had gotten all those boxes. I hauled her from room to room until her lies exposed the truth."

I nodded. Shit. I'd forgotten about those. "So she didn't just tell you?"

"Nope." Smoke curled from Van's nostrils.

Dot wasn't doing herself any favors, and now I understood why Van was convinced she was holding back more information.

"Well," Van continued, "it turns out there was a secret passage between that weird room with all the display cases and Ulric's old suite."

Hayden rubbed his eyes. "I don't know why I didn't know about that one, but I guess it makes sense. Both rooms used to be part of the alpha's suite."

Which was his parents' old suite.

"The warded seal on the door facing the hallway was unbroken, which is why Paws hadn't noticed anything wrong. But it's obvious someone's been in those rooms."

"I didn't even think to look for another entrance until I saw all the crap they'd hauled to the basement." Paws growled. "I've been trying to work out what's missing. Ulric had a list, but I haven't found it yet. And those stupid thieves made a mess of the place, so it's slow going. A whack of stuff is missing. Today I realized they even took the Jahaller, the bastards." Paws flicked his tail aggressively.

"What?" Van and Hayden shouted at the same time.

Dillon looked as confused as me.

"What's a Jahaller?" I asked.

"A small creature that defends home and hearth. They usually post themselves beside a fireplace," Van explained. "They look like small statues to most humans. Without supernatural interaction, they become more statue than creature until they are lost completely."

"He should have been safe in Ulric's room," Paws said. "The ward should have fed him enough magic to keep him going."

"Spells and curses, are you sure he's missing?" I asked, earning a hiss from Paws. "So he could be dying as we speak?"

"If he's with other supes, maybe not," Van said, rubbing the back of his neck. "And, well, if he's not, we need to find him soon, but the change doesn't happen right away—"

"He will not die," Paws said, swatting at Van to stop him from talking. "I won't allow it. We are going to find him and everything else those bastards took. Even if I have to go through Rob's pack lands inch by inch myself."

"They'd rip you apart up there," Hayden said, looking horrified by the idea of Paws trying to infiltrate Rob's pack.

"Don't underestimate me." Paws whipped his tail, then jumped off the table.

"How much do you think they got away with?" I asked.

Van scratched his head. "We found a few boxes when we searched the tunnel. It looks like they dropped them and ran when they realized we'd discovered their operation. But there are still at least two or three boxes unaccounted for, according to Dot." His tone suggested he didn't believe her, so he'd obviously scented a lie from her.

"And even more than that if they did that test run before, like they said they did," Dillon said.

Everyone frowned. That could be a lot of magical artifacts. How would we ever find them all? And if there were more things like that gramophone and the amulet, those artifacts could cause a lot of problems in the wrong hands. Speaking of which…

"What was up with that amulet and the gramophone anyway?"

"The best we can figure from what's left of the pendant is that it was capable of absorbing magic temporarily. So, when it was exposed to the gramophone, the stone absorbed the silencing magic it emitted. It probably wouldn't have lasted more than a day or so, but Robbie apparently had that all figured out and had recharged it after the attack at your apartment."

"It worked with any kind of magic?" Dillon asked.

Van nodded. "Apparently. Things could have been a lot worse if they'd figured that out."

Well. That was sobering.

"We were lucky Jake had that vision when he did," Hayden said.

"I should have looked more closely in the basement, even though Dot had already searched it. She was careful not to lie to me, and I hate that I didn't pick up on the weird way she was phrasing shit," Van said. "I didn't expect a fucking tunnel to be in there, though."

"You couldn't have known your deputy would betray you," Hayden said. "And it's my fault you didn't know about the tunnel. Never even thought about it, to be honest. My grandfather said it was closed after the end of the last shifter war. What was that, like 1906? I thought it'd caved in years ago. I'm not even sure how Robbie knew how to get into it from the other end."

"Well, they won't be getting into the inn through there again," I said.

I'd heard all about how a bunch of supes had gotten together to seal the tunnel properly this time. My brother had even helped when I'd kicked him out of my apartment for hovering and fussing too much. Magic and curses had been woven into the structure itself.

Jake brought us another round then, including another milk for me. I thanked him, even though I wished he'd snuck in a splash of Kahlua or something.

Then the conversations meandered to other, more mundane topics. As the night wore on, both humans and supes stopped by to say hi to me and welcome Dillon to the community. And I could see the moment Dillon started to understand why I'd wanted to come out tonight. Willow Lake was something special and with Dillon at my side, holding my hand, it was even better.

We even managed to talk to Van about our bond, showing off our newly minted fiery markings. He didn't have a lot of information, but suggested Doctor Roberts might have some answers. The fond way he said the doctor's name piqued my curiosity, but Van's love life wasn't really any of my business.

Tonight, I just wanted to be with Dillon. Tomorrow, we could worry about everything else.

The best part? At the end of the night, I knew exactly who I was going home with and who would hold me tight until morning.

And, by the end of the night, I realized maybe I belonged in Willow Lake more than I'd ever imagined.

THE END

Want to see what happens when Jeremy finds out about supes? ***Buy Jeremy's book, Wolves Always Bite***!

Not ready to say good-bye to Willow Lake yet? Join Lori's newsletter to receive regular emails with all my latest news and you'll also gain access to Willow Lake bonus content like a short story about Ash and Dillon and also ***Ravens Never Fall***, which is the prequel to this series. Set twelve years before ***Hellhounds Never Lie***, the prequel is a little bit sweet and a little bit sexy with Mercer and Oak falling in love while the pack falls apart.

———

WOLVES ALWAYS BITE

Willow Lake Supernaturals Book 2

What's a simple human to do when he discovers supernatural beings are real? Ask a LOT of questions, take a LOT of notes, and try to seduce a werewolf, of course!

Jeremy has always wanted to befriend mythical creatures, play with forbidden magic, and meet his fated mate. Okay, okay. He knows the different between fiction and real life, he is an author after all... Or he would be if he ever got to *The End* on one of his stories. So he knows his desire to live inside a fantasy romance novel is a touch unrealistic but where was the joy in living a life that was boring and predictable and overwhelmingly blah?

At least that's what he thinks until a hot AF werewolf saves him from his freaky boss and turns his whole life upside down. And his boss? She isn't the weird old lady he thought she was, but how could he have guessed she is a grumpy goblin with a reputation for selling black market magical artifacts? Now, Jeremy is determined to know *everything* about the supernatural world and Adrian, his swoon-worthy werewolf hero, is willing to answer *all* his questions, even when they make the big guy blush.

But when his former goblin boss kidnaps his cat to convince Jeremy to return the items she thinks he stole, things get serious fast. Now in between plotting his next MM romance and seducing the beautiful werewolf (and *not* just for research purposes), he needs to stage a cat rescue. Life is definitely not boring now.

Tags: *Jeremy has soooo many questions, Adrian tries to answer them even when they make him blush, no cats were* *hurt in the writing of this book, his best friend is a lying liar who lies, his book bag is his weapon of choice, don't touch the demon's dimples, supernaturals have magical everything, small towns aren't so bad especially when they are full of supernatural beings.*

Buy Wolves Always Bite now!

A Note from the Author

Hi!

Hey there! You're here! You've just finished book one of my first MM romance series. Yay! Thank you! I hope you enjoyed it!

I fell in love with MM romance several years ago and have read… well, um, a LOT of books in the genre since. Honestly, when I look at how many I've borrowed or purchased, the number is a little ridiculous. But, it's a better addiction than other things, right? However, when it came to writing one, I knew I'd need help. So, thank you to Kirk Waite at Rare Bird Beta Reading and to my editor June. You are both rockstars. But, as always, if any errors have survived to the final version, that's on me.

When I first thought about writing this series, Ash and Dillon were not in the picture. In fact, the first book I wrote about Willow Lake is Jake's story, which is now going to be book 3. So it took me a while to discover these two, but now I can't imagine the series starting any other way. I love Ash and his broken magic. I love Dillon and his search for a home. Willow Lake is the perfect place for them.

I'm sure you've already figured it out, but Jeremy's book is coming next. I am wildly excited to share it with you. His book has been a blast to write and will be releasing in November 2023. It is called **Wolves Always Bite** and you can pre-order it now.

And, I guess I should mention my newsletter! In addition to receiving my regular news and updates, subscribers also gain access to bonus content like a short story about Ash and Dillon and also **Ravens Never Fall**, which is the prequel for this series. Mercer and Oak fall in love just when everything else falls apart.

Okay, I think that's all I have for now! Wishing you a never ending supply of books you love! <3

Cheers,
Lori

PS… Reviews help other readers decide if a book might be something they want to read, so please consider writing a review of **Hellhounds Never Lie**. That would be wonderful and even Paws would be delighted.

About the Lori

When Lori was in elementary school, she wrote a very compelling story about a girl with a prickly personality who turned into a rose. (Sounds amazing, right? She knew you'd agree.) Then she discovered romances in her teens and, well, she knew she wanted to write romances. It took her a little longer to find MM romances, but once she did, she was addicted. She lives in a small town in Alberta with her husband and an elderly black cat.

Lori Ames writes MM romance with touch of magic!

You can find out more here:

- Facebook: facebook.com/LoriAmesAuthor
- Facebook Group: facebook.com/groups/LoriAmesReaders
- Website: loriames.com
- Newsletter: loriames.com/newsletter

Printed in Great Britain
by Amazon